to Jim
Hope you en[illegible]
the story.

un-changed

by

Gareth Sanderson

Introduction

The world has become a dark place in the last year But I am jumping into things. Let us go back to before…

The name is Stuart Lister. I am just your average-looking guy, nothing special to look at - short brown hair, green eyes, slim and just touching 6 foot. Life was going great. I was a student living in London with the most beautiful girlfriend, the best friends a man could ask for and I was studying to be a lawyer. Let us start when I met my girlfriend, Kimmy. I remember the first day she walked through the doors. I was sat at the back of the lecture theatre while Mr Balding was getting ready for class to start, and then she walked in and, somehow, it was just like in the movies. Everything slowed down and I felt I had all the time in the world to just look at her, stare at her rather. Her bright blonde hair glowed from the sun shining through the window, seeming to illuminate only her. She stopped and swept the room with her gaze, scanning everybody with her big blue eyes, then she finally got to me, saw me staring and gave me the biggest smile I have ever seen. My heart was pounding like it was trying to break my ribcage clean open, I had no idea what to do but time was playing tricks and suddenly she was beside me.

“Hi, I'm Kimmy.”

I just stared at her. It felt like forever had passed while Mr Balding had been shuffling his notes and setting up his PowerPoint. I must have freaked her out a little or she must have thought I was a bit stupid. Eventually a few words escaped me.

“Uh, Stuart, nice to meet you.”

From then on, we just clicked. Everything was working out perfectly; life could not have been better. And, naively, as you do on the cusp of twenty, I thought that my life would never go downhill, that, after we graduated, we would be happy together until the end of our days. We had plans to move out of the city and get jobs in a small law firm in a small town, living the life we both dreamed of. Looking back, it all sounded too perfect to ever come true.

So of course, life that happy could not continue. But it wasn't the normal story of growing apart, dissatisfaction with work and then each other. No, what happened to us was something you never thought would happen in the real world. It belonged to the reality of films or dreams, or so we thought.

It started small. First, the government found traces of another species living among us, lurking in the dark. Who knows how long they had been there, but they were there. At first everyone thought dismissed it as a group playing pranks or, more sinisterly, a cult pretending or believing they were something they were not. We stayed in denial a while longer but the truth could not be denied forever. Nobody wanted to call them what they really were because they did not want to admit that they were real, so we all took to calling them lurkers.

At first, we tried to reason with the lurkers and make a substitute for their food, and for a while it worked. But more and more people would begin to go missing every month and we humans began to feel more and more threatened as time went on. One morning, I lay in bed with Kimmy, watching the news. The government had declared a full country curfew to conduct a mass clear out of the lurkers. As humans, we were committed to stay indoors at night for the foreseeable future until the government thought it would be safe enough for us to reclaim the night. This strategy did not go as planned. A war had broken out between the lurkers and us, and suddenly, there were more of them than we ever could have imagined. We might have had greater numbers but they had the advantage of been faster, stronger and could use the dark to their advantage.

We were losing the war. The city felt especially unsafe so Kimmy and I decided to head out to her parents' house in Castleford. The day came when we were to set off. Then, as we were leaving the house, there was an earth-shattering explosion. Without warning us, without caring if we survived, the government had decided to level the main infected areas. That single blast killed thousands of both Lurkers and Humans. Our country was a battle ground, nothing but ruins. Kimmy and I survived the blast, living on the edge of the city, but we looked towards it and everything was rubble and dust. Contact with anybody else was impossible. Everything and everyone we knew had been obliterated in an instant and a new world had begun.

Chapter 1

After that blast, Kimmy and I lived for a time in a small cabin out in the middle of nowhere, miles from any town or city. We had walked for days to finally reach this oasis. Starving and dehydrated, our legs ready to give up, walking endlessly, I wanted to just lay down and give up but I had to stay strong for Kimmy. She was the only thing that kept me going, moving forward, despite the ache increasing more and more with every step. We searched for any scrap of food or drink to give us that extra bit of energy. Eventually, mercifully, the woods thinned out for a space, and in the distance, I saw a blur. My eyesight struggled to make out the object, dehydrated, light-headed and drowsy as I was, but with every step, it became clearer and clearer until I could finally see our salvation, a cabin in the middle of nowhere. In hindsight, another day walking would have defeated us. The cabin was just where we needed it to be, surrounded by woods on all sides and as isolated as it could be.

When we eventually crawled through the front door into the abandoned cabin, there did not appear to be any sign of a break in or forced entry. The owners must have left when the bombs were dropped. It looked like an old couple used to live here judging by the photos of an old man and women together and a family portrait with two little boys and a mother and father on a cabinet by the front door. They looked like a very happy family. Even in that state of exhaustion, and frequently over the course of the next months I wondered what became of them. After we scanned the front room quickly, we mustered up unknown reserves of energy and made it to the kitchen, pulling drawer after drawer open to find some sort of food, anything to keep us going. Thankfully, we found plenty of tinned food in the cupboards. I wasted no time in breaking several tins of soup open with a bread knife I found lying on the countertop, stabbing the top repeatedly until there was a sufficient hole and we could drink through it. We drank as much as we could until our stomachs resembled filled water balloons. Bloated and nauseous, we were so weak and drained from the journey that, as soon as we devoured what we could, we lay together entangled on the sofa and drifted into a more than needed sleep, a dreamless sleep.

When I woke up hours later, I remember looking around thinking how beautiful this little cabin was. Kimmy woke slowly after me and she agreed, we didn't want to change anything. Miraculously, this small cabin reminded us of the future we had wanted, and still wanted. In a way, we lived out that future together, in a small comfortable house in a field surrounded by woods, so secluded and quiet. Some days we could forget about what was happening out there. We were a world away. At night, you could hear animals in the woods creeping, snapping twigs and growling. For the first few days, these noises would frighten us, thinking there were lurkers hiding amongst the trees, trying to find fresh humans to eat. Eventually, like everything else, we got used to it and found it peaceful.

Before the rations of canned food ran out, I learned to hunt with the rifle I found on the top of the dresser in the old couples' bedroom. I guessed that it belonged to the old man before he had left and was glad that he had left it behind.

***

Ten months passed since the bombs dropped. Our refuge had become our home. We had not seen another soul this whole time although, there was an old brown five-door Escort in the drive, but I was too scared to leave the sanctuary that Kimmy and I had made for ourselves. While I wanted to know what was going on out there, whether our family and friends were still alive, it was too risky, I could not force myself to leave our idyllic home and the safety we found there.

The strong smell of gravy flowed from the kitchen where Kimmy was cooking. Before moving here, the only thing she could cook was beans on toast but now necessity had forced her to learn and experiment and she had become pretty good at it. She came walking into the living room holding steaming plates. I frequently get struck by how beautiful she was and how lucky I was that she picked me. Her fortitude had surprised us both, packed into her petite frame, only five foot. She knew how to dress to accentuate her curves. I was indeed a lucky man and sometimes I still just stared at her, rapt. Tonight, as she carried dinner in, she was wearing a blue jumper with a vee that showed her cleavage and tight jeans.

I could smell the freshly cooked rabbit, the taste buds in my mouth leaking saliva thinking about the tenderness of the meat and I could not wait to get stuck into it. I could not help but smile at her and say: "Let me guess, that lovely rabbit stew you are getting so good at?"

She looked at me as if I was being too cheeky.

"You should know what it is," she replied. "You caught it. You know you're getting pretty good at hunting now, hun."

Little did she know I had been in the woods for just over three hours and yet I had only caught a single rabbit. I let her believe that I was better than I actually was. I felt it made her feel safer. I would have stayed out longer in hope of catching another but it started to get dark and I did not want to risk it - the sound of the rifle shot was loud and it echoed in the forest, it could attract unwanted company.

I dug into the food and the rabbit was so soft and tender it just broke up in my mouth and slowly glided down my throat, filling my body with a comforting warmth.

"Oh, honey this is so good! I love you so much, but I'm starting to love your cooking a bit more."

She smiled in return and in mock annoyance said, "Hey you cheeky bugger!"

I felt so happy to be there with her, thinking that there was no one else I would rather be with.

I went into the kitchen to get a glass of water and just happened to look out of the window as the glass filled up. It was a small single glazed window, in an old style with four little glass panes surrounded by an old worn wooden frame. I thought I saw a quick glimpse of something in the distance, a shadow that quickly disappeared. I was not sure what I had seen or if I had seen anything but it made me a bit uneasy so I grabbed the rifle from the side where it was leaning up on the small cabinet near the front door with the pictures of the old couple and the family on it. We had never taken the photos down as it cheered us up to look at them sometimes, seeing how happy they were together. I took the rifle to the table with me, which made Kimmy nervous, her eyes dropping down to the rifle.

“Is everything okay, Stuart?”

“Yeah it’s fine babe, just a precaution, trying to be safe like usual, you know me.”

It did not help and I saw her get uneasy herself and clench her knife and folk tighter. Everything seemed to go completely quiet, I could not hear the birds outside or even the draft of the gentle wind beneath the door. Everything just seemed to stop. I placed the glass down on the table and began to sit down and then a sudden bang from outside brought us both to our feet, Kimmy jumping up and across to grab my arm tightly. I quickly backed her into the corner of the room where there were no windows and stood in front of her readying the rifle.

“Stuart, what was that?”

“I don't know.”

A few seconds passed but our adrenaline was still high.

“I'm scared, Stuart.”

“It’s gonna be fine, babe, don’t worry, I won’t let anyone touch you.”

I pointed the rifle at the door. Other than the bang, there had been no other noise and now it was eerily quiet again. All I could hear was the heavy breathing of Kimmy behind me, every second making me more and more tense. The hair on the back of my neck stood on end. The sounds from Kimmy suddenly stopped as she held her breath. I realised that I was holding mine too. Then, the door flew open. I let off a shot automatically and we both fell back with the shock and recoil of the shot. I should have been used to the recoil but I was so tense, I fell backwards and felt Kimmy grab me even tighter. Trying to keep myself together, I quickly reloaded the rifle and pointed it at the door, waiting for a second attempt of entrance from who or whatever was out there, but nothing happened. It was quiet again. I made a move to get up but Kimmy pulled me back.

"What are you doing?" she whispered.

"I've got to take a look. Stay here."

I crept slowly towards the door as Kimmy quivered in the corner. The wooden floorboards creaked with every step I took. I reached the door and looked outside but there was nothing there. It was far too quiet. I turned around slowly and, before I knew it, I was grabbed and thrown across the room. I dropped the rifle and then crashed into the table which collapsed over me. I wasted no time, grabbed the sharp knife we had been using for dinner from the floor, amongst the wreckage of the table and ran towards the man heading for Kimmy. He grabbed me by the throat before I could even swing my arm. He was so powerful; I couldn't knock his arm loose - it was like a solid piece of wood holding me by the throat. I could feel all the blood boiling in my head as he strangled me, his fangs shining with saliva, looking all the world like a rabid animal ready to attack. His eyes shone with a bright green light, and my head felt as if it was going to pop off. As I looked into those mesmerising green eyes, my vision began to fade and my breath was ragged, trying to get through my block airways. At that moment, the thought came to me that if I die here so does Kimmy and with that thought another rush of energy flowed through me, giving me the strength to throw the knife with some force towards his head, hoping for the best before I passed out. Miraculously, it hit his eye at an angle to stick. In shock and pain, screaming inhumanly, he let go of me. Coughing and choking, I tried to breathe as freely as I could, beckoned to Kimmy to go ahead of me so I could protect her and we both ran together out of the front door, grabbing the car keys from the sideboard and leaving our attacker screaming in pain. We ran down the pebble drive to the car that we had never used. We knew that driving at night would attract attention but, in that moment, it did not seem to matter. I had to get us out of there. When Kimmy was safely in the passenger's seat, I ran to the driver's seat, started the car up and set off as fast as I could causing a wheel spin as we set off. We flew along the dirt tracks trying to get to an open road where we were not surrounded by forests on each side which no longer felt safe, not knowing what could be in there. I looked over at Kimmy who was still pale and shivering, staring right ahead into the darkness.

"Are you ok?" I asked gently. She did not reply just sitting there shivering, her face pure terror. Keeping one hand on the wheel, I reached for her shoulder.

"Kimmy, babe, look at me."

She took a deep breath, grounded herself and looked at me. I could still see that fear in her face. It almost made me break down myself knowing how scared she must have been. I could feel my eyes getting ready to fill with tears, but I had to stay strong for her, so I turned my head back to the road to focus and stop the tears from coming out. I gathered myself and then went straight back to Kimmy.

"Kimmy, you're safe, we've got away. You're with me, I told you I wouldn't let anyone hurt you."

She looked at me for a while her eyes welled up but then she could not hold it in any longer and she burst into tears crying, flinging her arms around me. While keeping my eyes on the road, I used my other arm to comfort her.

"I thought you were gonna die. I thought he was gonna kill us."

I squeezed her tighter to let her know I was there and that we were safe. I began to feel her calm down, her body began to loosen up and the shivering stopped.

"We're gonna be fine, babe, everything's gonna be ok."

We finally came to something that looked like a main road. I slowed down a bit, trying to work out which way should we go and there were not any signs to help. I had no idea where we should go. Everything we had known for the last 10 months was in that cabin and now our home was gone. I did not even know which county we were in.

The junction was coming up quickly and with a quick turn of my arm we were suddenly heading left, hoping that that meant north. I had no idea where this road would take us but I could not stop in the middle of nowhere to think about it. We were safest when on the move, locked in the car. I kept scanning the sides of the road hoping to see a sign that would help but all I could see was darkness in the forest, and the more I looked the more I kept feeling like I was seeing things in there. I was so tired and scared that it could just have been my mind playing tricks on me, but I didn't want to stop and sleep in case the shapes and shadows were real. The moment I stopped, something could make its move on us.

I looked towards Kimmy and she was staring out the window probably wondering the same as me: thoughts of what we should do, where we should try to make a new sanctuary. Our home had yet again been taken from us and we had no idea where we were. I felt like I should say something comforting to her, but what could I say. I was at just as much of a loss as she appeared to be.

I saw her eyes light up as she pointed ahead of us, saying, "Look, Stuart."

I focused ahead trying to see what stood in our way, but then I saw a sign welcoming us to Luton and realised we must be on the M1 motorway which leads to Yorkshire. We had driven this road before. It goes straight up to Castleford where Kimmy's parents live. I allowed myself to feel some relief knowing where we were. I glanced over at Kimmy who had a particular smile on her face that could cheer anyone up in the worst of situations.

"My parents, oh my God, Stuart, what if they're still in Castleford?"

I didn't want her to think the worst, I wanted her to enjoy this feeling, so I stayed clear of any negativity.

"I know babe, they probably are. You know your dad; he would never leave if he knew there was even a chance of you showing up."

"I've missed them so much. I hope they're still there and they didn't get run out by those monsters."

I forced a laugh to help her feel more at ease.

"I would love to see one of those things up against your dad. He's like a silverback gorilla, they'd probably run from him if they saw him charging at them."

She let out this small giggle and I saw a few tears trickle out as she did, not from sadness but from happiness and that little bit of hope that she might be able to see her family again. It made me feel so happy to see her like that, even for a short while, it would have been worth it.

I never want her to lose that smile. Every time I see it, it reminds me of just how much I love her. I suddenly thought of the funny moment when I first met her dad, and was quick to remind her.

"I remember when you first took me back to yours babe, and your dad didn't like me."

She laughs. "Course he did, don't be stupid."

"Oh yeah? When we first met and shook hands, he nearly broke my fingers."

"He does that with everyone to see if they have a manly shake. He likes his men to be men, you know that."

"I do, I remember the disappointment in his face, when I said I didn't do any sports. He looked at me like I had just kicked him in the balls."

Kimmy let out a huge laugh that moved her whole body, she knew exactly how her dad felt about me - he hated the fact that I was stealing his little beautiful princess away. She had been a major daddy's girl when she was younger, so you can imagine what he was like when she finally brought a boy back to meet her parents. He was a scary man, over 6 foot, as wide as a train, and a presence that made me feel he was towering over me. He got me alone the first time I met him and said to me in that deep Yorkshire accent, "Listen, lad, if you hurt my little girl, these hands, well, they ain't crushed anything in a while, if ya get what I'm saying…"

I genuinely felt like I needed to take a leak when he said that to me but I buckled up and replied, "I won't hurt her, sir, I love her." It seemed to be the right response as he then gave me a pat on the back that nearly knocked me to the floor - it was a welcome to the family pat, I assumed.

Kimmy let out a big yawn and I could see that she was getting tired but probably didn't want to go to sleep thinking, if she did, she would be leaving me on my own. But she needed her rest after what we had just been through. We both did but I knew I couldn't sleep until we were in the north.

"Get some sleep, hun, we will be able to reach Castleford in a few hours."

"I don't want to leave you to drive up with no company."

"Don't worry about me, babe, I'm fine. I want you to get some rest."

I reached over with my left arm, pulled her head towards mine and gave her the softest kiss. It sent a warm and comfortable feeling through my body. I could stay like that forever, her arms went around my neck and she moved towards me, leaning over the gear stick, tightening her lips to mine, but I had to let her sleep so I pulled away, gave her another kiss on the forehead and let her close her eyes.

After a while, I looked to the fuel gauge and realised the light was on. It wasn't going to last until Castleford, we would need to stop to fill up the tank, but I did not want to worry her with this yet, so I let her sleep. I could at least let her have a peaceful hour before we had to stop.

Chapter 2

It was pitch black and there was no noise, silent to the point that I could hear my own heartbeat. I had been driving for what felt like forever but, in reality, it had only been a little under 2 hours. My eyes were feeling as heavy as if two pieces of stone were attached to them pulling them down. Kimmy was fast asleep; she looked so peaceful with her cheek resting on her hands tucked underneath and she was making little snoring noises, not a real snore, just a little cute snort as her breathing would catch every now and then. I tried to focus on the sound of her breathing to stay awake but it was so rhythmic, it was lulling me to sleep. I used to tease her about those noises all the time - she would never believe me when I told her that she snored, she would get so defensive and embarrassed. Then, she would try to give me the silent treatment to make me feel bad for teasing her, but I knew all I had to do to make her feel better was to stroke the inside of her arm with my fingertips. She loves that. I would do it whenever she was upset, even at the smallest things. Sometimes I think she would pretend to be more upset than she actually was just so I would stroke her arm.

As I felt myself falling asleep at the wheel, I knew this was not good but the worry was not enough to boost the chemicals in my brain and keep me awake. Looking at the fuel gauge did not help. It was almost empty and I knew this was bad but still my eyelids drooped and I struggled to concentrate on the road. I debated playing some music but Kimmy looked so peaceful, I could not purposefully wake her. I shook my head and slapped my cheeks hoping the little rush would wake me up slightly. I tried to focus on the immediate problem: we were going to need to stop soon in the middle of the night or, if we kept going in the hope that we could last until the sun came up, eventually we would break down. We would need to stop. I could not risk breaking down before the sun came up and being stranded and obvious on the motorway. I drove on, looking for a good place to lie low.

I saw an outline of something in the distance. At first, it looked like a mirage, my mind playing tricks on me from the lack of sleep, but, as I drove closer, the outline became more distinct. Finally, we had reached a petrol station at the side of the road. I started to slow and indicate. Either the tick of the indicator or the slowing of the car woke Kimmy and she looked around perplexed as we came to a full stop.

"What's going on? Why have we stopped?" she asked frantically, her nerves rising as she woke and remembered what had happened.

I pointed at the station, "We need gas, hun. We are nearly out."

"Ya can't get out of the car. Just keep driving Stuart," she said with a straight face.

"Kimmy, darling, if I just keep going now, we are gonna run out of gas, and god knows where we will break down, or even if it will be light when we do."

I could see the fear in her eyes as she looked towards me. Her lips trembled. She knew that we had to do this, but she still needed some convincing.

"Babe, I will be in and out. We just need to fill the tank so it can last all the way to Castleford."

Her hands began to shake so I grabbed them to pull her towards me and hugged her so tight.

I whispered consolingly into her ear, "It looks abandoned. It doesn't look like anybody has been here for months, it'll be okay. We need to do this, babe."

She eventually nodded her head in agreement, so I shifted the gear into first and slowly rolled into the station trying to make as the least noise possible from the engine. We rolled up to the side of the pumps but I hesitated for a moment. I took a deep breath and, from the safety of the car, I took a good look around as my heart started to beat harder and faster, wondering what I was doing. My hands began to tremble so I clenched my fists to suppress my fears. I peered into the darkness in all directions and I could see nothing around at all. This did not calm me as I was well aware that, being so dark, I could only see so far into the distance, and anything could be lurking beyond. I peered into the building and could not see anything but stacked shelves. The wind blew gently and it looked as safe as it could so I opened the door and ran around to the pump, grabbed it and realized that, with the fear of it all, I had forgotten to open the fuel cap, so I ran back to the door and pulled the lever that flicks the cap open. I almost dropped the lid as I was opening it. I put the pump in and pulled, taking another good look around as it filled up. Only hearing the wind blowing gently, a dry leaf sliding across the ground and the ticking of petrol flowing through the pump, I let a huge sigh of relief run through my body. As the tank filled, I felt a little better about the decision that I had made. It was almost over and if anything was waiting for me, surely it would have attacked by now? With what I had heard of the lurkers from the news from the days before all hell broke loose, they are not ones to wait around. They are beasts who attack instantly on sight like rabid animals. From my own experience a few hours before, I had no grounds to dismiss this idea. The growl he released as he grabbed me was loud and shook his whole body in rage, there was no humanity left. That lurker was a beast, nothing more. The meter now read 30 pounds worth of petrol, which should easily be enough to get to Castleford and beyond, so I finished up, put the pump back and ran back around to jump in the driver's seat, still shaking from the adrenaline. I paused a second to look once again into the building. I definitely could not see anything alive in there.

"What are you waiting for? Start the car up!" Kimmy snarled. But I have an idea and I cannot shake it out. I should get some supplies whilst we still have the chance. We would not stop again.

"I'm gonna go in."

"What? What are you talking about? Why would you do that?"

"We don't know what's going to happen, we need supplies in case it takes longer than we think to reach there. We need some food and drink." I did not say that we needed supplies in case something had happened to her parents, in case we needed to keep going, in case Castleford no longer existed. She did not need to spend the rest of the journey fearing what we might find when we reached our destination.

She grabbed my arm and squeezed it so tight that it almost hurt. "Please Stuart, let's just go. We can take the risk. I don't mind being a bit hungry."

"I can't take that risk, Kimmy. Not when it comes to you. Stay in the car. I will be fast, I promise."

I started to walk away but she leaned forward and grabbed my arm again, pulling my face towards hers. "Please be careful. I love you, Stuart."

She was so scared, nearly in tears again, and this time it was my fault, because of my decision to go in. I felt so guilty, but that was tempered with the thought of what if we got to Castleford and nobody was there? I could not pass up the chance to have food stocked in the car in case we needed it.

"I love you too, babe," I said before silently jogging to the main door. I tried to look through the glass but it was covered in dust and humidity and all I could see was the outline of shelves as I had seen from the car. I wiped the glass with my sleeve and gazed through the circle I made. It was dark but I could see inside more clearly now and could make out the rows of tinned food, crisps and drinks on the shelves, ours for the taking. I tried the door and it seemed my luck was holding out as it was open. I slowly pulled open and, as the hinges were so stiff from underuse, it stayed open. Sneaking in, I grabbed a basket and started throwing tins inside, not caring what was inside as long as it would be edible. As I was picking up water bottles from a fridge that was warm enough that it felt as if it had not been on for a long while now, I looked saw medicines and plasters behind the counter . Who knew if we would need them but I shot over and took several packs of tablets and plasters to be on the safe side. As I was chucking the boxes into the basket, I noticed a glint in my peripheral vision and spun around. Some metal was reflecting what little light there was under the counter. Without hesitation, I reached for it and pulled it out: a silver six shot revolver. I examined it, twisting it around in the moonlight which caused rays of light to shine around the dark room. It looked pristine and as if it worked so I wasted no time and tucked it into the waistband of my jeans. Happy with the supplies I had, I made my way towards the door. Suddenly, I heard the cock of a gun and I came to a halt. It sounded like the cock of a shotgun or a rifle and I registered this, immediately alert, as all the hair on my body stood on end and a chill ran down my spine. I froze knowing that I could be dead in any second. Then a deep voice said, "Whatcha doing in here?"

I turned around slowly and looked at the man who was threatening me. He was a small man with grey hair, and looked to be in his fifties. He was pointing a large rifle straight at my head from no more than four feet away from me but I had not heard him approach and was being so quiet myself. I looked in his eyes. They shone in the night as if he had two little lights behind each one, which could only mean that he was a lurker. But if he was a lurker, why would he have a gun? And why had he not already attacking me? I was frozen to the spot, unable to open my mouth, or move in any way, terrified, staring.

"I asked you a question lad. Answer me!" he shouted, making me jump which thankfully brought me back in control of my body. Kimmy must have noticed something was wrong, watching from the car because she started screaming my name as she jumped out the car and came running towards the building. I could not let her come in so I shouted in her direction, without my eyes leaving the man with the gun.

"Kimmy, stay out there now, don't come in." He had aimed his gun towards her so I slowly and gently, moved myself into the path to protect her as I answered: "I'm sorry sir, point it at me instead please, we just needed some supplies, we're hungry, we didn't think anybody was here." I was begging, thinking how hopeless it was to beg - like begging a hungry wolf not to eat you.

His eyes merely glared at me so I continued pleading with him, "You can have your stuff back, sir, just don't hurt her, please."

Kimmy had stayed outside but she was in plain view of the man. My heart was racing, my eyes started to warm up. These I could be our last minutes and there would be nothing I could do. I was still exhausted, desperately needed to sleep and rest and was in no fit state to fight someone supernaturally stronger than me. This man was clearly a lurker and yet something did not quite fit. Why had he not tried to eat me yet? The last lurker, just a few hours ago, had not waited. That one had not spoken. Surely, we should already be dead. Lurkers did not wait and point guns at humans.

His eyes switched back and forth from one of us to the other, scanning us with those cold bright eyes.

"You're human," he said. Then I realised that he must have the gun to fight off other lurkers. Now he knew that we were human, he was going to kill us for certain. I didn't know what to say and could not focus on words. My body felt stiff as a tree and yet I could hear the gentle rattle from the metal basket and tins banging against each other caused by my hands shaking. I could do nothing but look at him, waiting for what was about to come, berating myself as all I had to do was keep on driving and not come into this shop and then Kimmy would not be in this situation, we would be safe in the car far away from this man. Why did I have to come in? Kimmy was right; why didn't I listen to her?

Then, to my surprise, he lowered the gun. My heart began racing even faster as I waited for him to attack without it. He did not need a gun as we were not a threat. I looked to see tears streaming from Kimmy's eyes. She mouthed, "I love you" to me as she sobbed. If I distracted him for long enough, Kimmy could still make it to the car. I could try to fight him for just long enough for her to escape. I had to do something. I felt so guilty as it was my decision that had landed Kimmy here. She would not have to pay for my idiotic mistake. I tensed, lowered the basket gently, and slowly reached around to the revolver tucked into my jeans, ready for action, ready to give him everything I had so that Kimmy could get out of there. Before I had touched the cold metal of the gun, "go." He almost whispered the word.

I was so shocked, I just looked back at him for a moment before saying, "What?"

"Take the food and go."

I opened my mouth to speak but had no words. It crossed my mind that this could be a sort of trick, a way to torment me, playing with me like a child or cat playing with its food. Then he shouted again, "Go, before I change my mind!"

This time, I saw the fangs as clear as day, saliva shimmering on the white enamel in the moonlight. I wasted no time and ran out of the door, grabbed Kimmy with the hand not carrying the basket and threw us both and all the groceries into the car, scattering tins and boxes over the floor. I started the engine and we hurtled away. I had driven a little way down the road before Kimmy broke down. She started slapping my arm and then anywhere she could read on my body. I slammed on the brakes so that she could have her fit of rage at me safely.

"I told you not to go in! Why didn't you listen?" she snarled at me.

She was flapping her hands as a flamingo would its wings. I caught them and held them tight to my chest to calm her down. I knew she was acting like this from the fear of watching someone point a gun at me. I cradled her in my arms, rocking her gently to lull her as her whole body shook and she sobbed loudly. My feelings of guilt resurged. I had put her through that. It was my fault she was upset. I cradled her head for a moment before gently raising her face to look me.

"Kimmy, sweetheart, look at me." Her eyes burned red from all the tears but she looked up at me doe-eyed and calmer. I used my shirtsleeve to wipe the tears away.

"I am so sorry for putting you through that. I will never let that happen again. The last thing I want to do is see you hurt, I love you so much. I'm so sorry." I always better at calming her with my actions, I struggled to know what to say. Regardless, she flung herself onto me, kissing me. I was surprised for a second but returned her kisses fervently, our lips pushing harder against each other. My heart was still racing from our ordeal and now it had a new reason to beat yet faster. I could not help myself and grabbed her tighter, managing to pull her on top of me in the driver's seat. She sat on top of me as we continued to kiss, our bodies providing friction through our clothes as we did. After all the years we have been together, I still get butterflies when we touch like it is the first time. I ran my lips down to her neck and pulled her hair back gently. She ran her hands underneath my shirt and rubbed my chest as I pulled her top off and started to stroke her body. Then I kissed her stomach and rubbed my hands down her back; she pushed me hard against my seat and started to loosen my belt. The moment was intense and I felt more alive and present than in months. I could feel the excitement palpably running through the both of us. As she began to unzip my jeans, we heard a scream from down the road. It sounded like an echo from a distance.

In an instant, we stopped what we were doing and stared down the road behind us, Kimmy staring ahead from where she sat on my lap and me craning my neck behind. For a while, we stared, our breath still heavy. As much as we wanted to keep going, we knew we were not safe, sat here in the middle of the road out in the open. We had not driven far from the petrol station after all. So I took a few deep breaths and Kimmy climbed off me, clumsily, back into the passenger's seat. Our hearts were pounding and apparently all the excitement and horror of our situation did wonders for our appetite for one another. She let out a little giggle, muttering, "stupid idea" between the giggles. I too decided to laugh it off, letting out a chuckle as I refastened my jeans and belt and restarted the ignition but left it idle for a moment as I watched Kimmy.

Hooking her bra back together with one hand, she picked her blue jumper from the dashboard and pulled it back over her head. I watched her sorting herself out, checking herself in the mirror adjusting her hair and smoothing her eyebrows and could not help but laugh again, this time less forced. She shot me daggers.

"What?"

I grinned. "I just love that even with the world in ruins, our brush with death, and any number of things behind us, you still have to look your best."

She nudged my arm, "Shurrup you."

I couldn't help but continue to tease her to lighten the mood and distract myself. "Oh, hun, you've got a bit of something on ya lip."

She frowned at the mirror.

"Where?"

"Just there, right side of your top lip."

"I can't see anything! Where?"

I laughed again. "I'm just joking with you, babe."

She shut put the mirror back up with force "Knob-head. Start the car and let's get out of here."

So I shifted gear, brought the car to the bite point and we rolled off down the road.

"After all that, what did you get?" Kimmy asked as she dived into the basket, collecting the tins which had rolled onto the floor. She pulled out a packet of cheese and onion crisps, opened them with an uncomfortably loud pop and dug into them. She fed me some while I kept my eyes on the road, driving away from the scream we had heard and towards what I hoped was safety.

Kimmy seemed relaxed though, pulling out a bottle of water, opening it up and draining nearly half the bottle in one gulp. She relaxed onto my shoulder and, safely in fourth gear, I took my hand of the gearstick and put my arm around her. The events of this night seemed unreal and far away from us in the safety of the car. The whole of our last year seemed unreal.

"Remember the things we used to worry about this time last year. Back when we were still at university. God, imagine telling us then that we'd be fleeing from lurkers, driving through the night."

Kimmy let out a little sigh. "Yeah, all we had to worry about were essay deadlines and exams."

I turned to kiss her head as I laughed. "We used to think it was the end of the world a couple days before hand in. Well you did."

Kimmy jumped away from me.

"Me?! What about you? You'd nearly chew your own hand off sitting at that laptop, staring at your assignments!"

I thought back, remembering just how terrible I was when it came to dealing with deadlines and couldn't help but laugh. Kimmy started to laugh with me and then laid back down on my shoulder and said gently: "It was all kind of stupid when you look back. I would definitely swap man-eating monsters for essay deadlines in a heartbeat."

I rested my head on hers and thought back to the day I first asked her out. It was on a deadline day during our first semester. I was stressing out in class worried that my assignment was not good enough to pass. I felt horrible and was so nervous that I was shaking. I must have looked a right mess. Then she walked in and, as with every time I saw her that semester, I couldn't help but smile. Her presence calmed me and made every bad thought in my head go away. I could block it all out by concentrating on how beautiful she looked and hoping she would come over. My heart would speed up even from when she glanced briefly at me. This time, she did come over to me.

"So how badly did you want to shoot ya self last night?" She said it so casually it took a moment for the words to sink in. I think my laugh in response might have been a bit of an overreaction but I don't think she minded. She gave me another of her dazzling smiles. I buckled up my courage as I never thought that she would say yes: "Um, Kimmy, seeing as we've got this essay out of the way now, do you maybe want to celebrate with a drink or a meal or something?"

I was terrified she would say no and thought that if she did, I would die of embarrassment. I should have asked her out in private or online, but she looked at me and said, "I would love to go out with you, Stuart."

A few of our classmates wolf-whistled but I did not care. I was so happy, I nearly jumped up in joy but I tried to keep my cool and not show her how much of a geek I was.

She made everything I had been through up to that point worthwhile. Everything, no matter how awful, had led me to her. I could never regret a single thing about my life because anything had changed, I would never have gone to this university and met Kimmy.

My family had abandoned me when I was little. I went into the system and bounced from foster home to foster home, never settling in any, never having a proper family. I was brought up more by my social worker than anyone else and she would tell me about her time at university, although I am sure she censored parts to tell a teenager. It would be so interesting to listen to her stories. They were the best years of her life and I wanted the same. I firmly decided, that despite my disadvantages, I was going to study as hard as I could so that as soon as I came of age, I would go to university and create a life for myself as an adult. In the future I pictured, I never imagined a woman as beautiful, as funny and as smart as Kimmy. Truth be told, before I met her, I had never really pictured any girl in my future.

I leant down to kiss her on the head and breathed in enjoying that beautiful smell of coconut and lavender which lingered in her hair from the last time she bathed in the cabin. I fervently hoped that when we reached Castleford, we would find her family safe and well, that the worst had not happened. I could not bear to watch her go through that kind of pain. It would be horrible.

And we should be there in an hour or so.

I had drifted into reverie. A shape in the road jolted me out and I refocused. Suddenly there was somebody there in the middle of the road. I slammed on the brakes as quickly as possible and Kimmy went flying into the dashboard. I swerved abruptly but I still heard a thump and saw a dark shape roll over the bonnet. My swerve spun us across the road. I pulled up the handbrake and held Kimmy with one arm while squeezing the steering wheel with the other until we came to a stop.

"Kimmy, are you ok? Are you hurt?" I screamed in fear and shock.

She came to, slowly. She looked a little spaced out and had a little red mark on her forehead from where she had hit the dashboard

I repeated myself, "Kimmy, are you ok?"

"I'm fine, I think, just banged my head. What happened?"

"I hit somebody. I swerved to try miss them but I hit them anyway."

I looked to where they slouched in the dark, a woman with long black hair. She was looking at the car but I could not tell if she was alright, or if she was even human for that matter. It was far too dark. After my last excursion, I was hesitant to leave the safety of the car but I could not leave a human to die on the street. I was never the type to hit and run. I undid my seatbelt and told Kimmy to stay where she was but, when I looked back to see the woman, she was gone. My brain went into overdrive a I realised what that meant.

"She's a lurker!" I shouted as I tried to start the car up again but before I knew it the door swung open and she grabbed me, crushing my shoulder as she did and she flung me out of the car and over the road. I landed on my back, causing a jarring pain to shoot up me. As it faded, my whole back stung as if landing on the ground had scraped all the skin from my back. I could hear Kimmy screaming for the lurker to stay away from me but, before I knew it, she picked me off the ground and held me up. I looked into her face. This one clearly was not going to let us walk away unharmed. Her eyes were black as the night and did not shine like the others I had seen tonight. She made such horrid noises, a kind of animalistic growling like a predator ready to strike its prey. My body was in so much pain from the throw I could barely move. I tried squirming but my muscles were unable to make the slightest movement. Still holding me, she sniffed me like a human would smell a pot of food to see if it was ready. Then, I remembered the gun tucked into my jeans, no doubt causing part of the pain from being thrown to the tarmac. With what strength I had left, I tried to grab it but, before I could, she growled loudly and, with her inhuman speed, thrust her fangs into my right shoulder. I could feel the blood flowing out of my body. My vision went hazy but the pain slowly dissipated too. I felt myself weaken and it was almost peaceful. Fuzzily, I could feel my self dying, like fading away into a deep sleep, numb. Nevertheless, thoughts of Kimmy kept me tethered to life for a moment more. The worst thing was that she had to watch me die and I knew the same fate awaited her as soon as this beast had finished with me. In my numb, half-paralysed state, I seemed to be flailing and felt my hand brush something hard and metallic. The gun. Some sense of self kicked in and adrenaline coursed through my veins again. With this new energy, I raised the gun from my jeans and I pulled the trigger once, twice, three times right into her chest. My vision was almost gone but it was such close range I could not miss. She dropped me and I fell to the floor like a rag doll. I tried to raise my head but I had used up my last reserve of energy. I faded in and out. She was now also fallen to the floor, screaming in pain and clutching her chest. I had no idea if that was going to kill her so I knew I needed to move; I needed to get us out of there but my body was so drained it felt like I was covered by a sheet of metal, trapped beneath it and only my head could move and that still felt like lead, so hazy and heavy. Thoughts came slowly but still I tried to get up. My muscles barely responded and I just fell back to the ground. I had nothing left to give, I was all out of fight. I just wanted to scream to Kimmy "get out of here now, get out of here before she gets back up." I did not know if the words came out of my mouth or not but I thought them as forcefully as I could, screamed them within my own head before everything went black. As I drifted away, I clung to hoping to hear the screech of the car before I passed out. All I could hear were the horrid screams of the lurker. I hoped beyond hope that Kimmy would get away before she got back up.

Then suddenly I did feel something through the haze. I was getting dragged across the floor. I thought it was the lurker trying to finish me off so I tried to fight back but it was useless, my body was done, I had nothing left to give. Then my vision clearer slightly for a quick second and I saw a blur of blue. Kimmy. Kimmy was somehow dragging me across the road. I faded in and out. Then somehow, she had got me into the back of the car. I tried to keep my eyes open, tried to keep them fixed on Kimmy but my eyelids were just too heavy and everything went black.

Chapter 3

A very tall man with brown hair and wearing a cotton brown jumper walks through the field with a short black-haired woman. They head straight into the middle of the field but suddenly the man stops dead and stretches his arm out across to stop the woman.

"Stop," he says gently, almost whispering. "Do you hear that."

The woman listens intently. Both their heads spin to the left, quickly and in unison, hearing the noise of an animal burrowing in the mud next field over. Human ears could not hear that.

Both their eyes shine bright in the night as if two little bulbs shine behind them, giving them perfect night vision. These are two lurkers hunting in the moonlight.

"Are you ready for this, Cassandra?" the man whispers.

She looks at him and nods.

"This one is yours. I will go further into the fields to find my own."

The man sprints off in the opposite direction at a non-human speed. In the space of a few seconds, he is gone. The woman lowers herself down to nearly all fours and starts to creep through the field, ghost-like and silent. She draws closer, getting the animal in her sights and realises that it is a helpless little fox. She inches closer and closer without the fox having the slightest clue that it is been hunted by master predator.

She smells the air, taking in its scent and storing it to memory. Less than fifty yards away, she analyses the fox then drops down yet lower into a pose where she is ready to strike, to pounce like a cat. Her eyes pierce the animal, already imagining the kill. She darts off at a speed impossible to follow with the human eye. The fox jumps from the sudden approach and jets off across the field, trying desperately to keep in front of the lurker, darting from side to side to shake her off. After a minute of chasing, the lurker has gained on the fox and is almost ready to attack the poor defenceless animal, but they are both moving too fast. They come to a motorway at the edge of the field and the fox tears across the road with the lurker at its heels, fingers inches from its tail then a screech and a smash, and the lurker hurdles over the bonnet of a car and is sent flying in the air.

The male lurker hears the screech and the smash from where he hunts two fields away. He pauses, listening intently to decipher where from the source of the noise is and then sprints towards it. As he vaults over the border hedges, he hears gun shots, shouts in a man's voice, desperately telling his partner to save herself, screams of pain from what sounds like Cassandra. He stops at the bank before the road, peering over the top to see a young attractive woman trying to pull a young man who looks unconscious into the back off the car. The lurker is about to set off to check on Cassandra when he catches a glimpse of the young man's face in the light from the interior of the car. This stops him in his tracks. His face drops in a harsh realisation. He knows this young man, knows him well in fact, has been watching him from a distance, watching him from his boyhood, lurking at the edges, as he grew into the man he can see now being pulled into the car by his girlfriend. This is the boy he has been keeping safe for years, making sure the boy's life was full without him, the watcher, in it.

He snaps back to reality as the car zooms away down the motorway. He runs to his friend and digs the bullets from her body with his fingernails, causing her to stop screaming and her wounds to heal over. Before she can thank him, he lifts her into the air by her collar and screams at her: "What did you do?"

The fear on her face shows all too well. She is very afraid; she has never seen her friend lash out so quickly. He usually takes a lot to anger. He always searches for the good in people and gives second chances. Why not this time, she asks herself.

He screams again in frustration.

"I'm sorry, Richard!" she screeches back at him. "I lost control when the car hit me - my hunger and anger took over. I am not as strong as you, it's not easy to just stop drinking human blood like that Richard, especially when it is easy prey."

He ignores her statement and stares into her eyes.

"Did you hurt the boy?"

He says trying desperately to hold back some of his fear of what she may have done to him. She says nothing, just looks to him with sorrow and regret in her eyes.

"Did you kill him, Cassandra?" he shouts at her.

"No!" she screams back. "He got away and he shot me, didn't he? Does that not get me off the hook? He shot me!"

He lets her go and she falls to the ground before gingerly getting up and dusting herself off as he paces back and forth.

"No, it does not. We do not feed upon humans, Cassandra. You have not touched human blood for months. You've done well. Why break that streak now? Why with this boy?"

"I told you, I lost control when they hit me with the car."

"You are lucky you didn't kill him, Cassandra, as much as a friend you are to me. God save you, I wouldn't have been able to stop."

"Why?" she screams. "What is special about this boy and not any of the others I have hurt in the past?"

"Because he's my son!" he screams in her face.

She is lost for words and just stares into his saddened eyes.

He stares away into the distance for a moment before beginning to speak.

"I lost track of him when the bombs dropped. I couldn't track his scent. After searching for a while, I assumed he was dead, so I stopped searching and came back to town to keep helping."

She walks up behind him. "Oh, so that's why you went missing for all that time," she says gently.

The silence becomes awkward and intense and she tries to say something but her voice chokes up. He spins around to look at her as she tries to get the words out.

"What is it?" he asks her.

She finally opens her mouth and the truth comes out in a rush. "I bit him, Richard. I bit your son."

His face drops with pure terror, eyes wide and haunted. "You what? No, no. How could you do this Cassandra? No." He sets off down the road and she stops him before he has taken a few steps.

"Where are you going?" she asks.

"I need to get to him. Rotherham is the next town. If they stop there, I could get to him in time. I need to help him."

"You can't, Richard," she yells, stopping him again.

He faces her straight on. "Yes, I can. You have ruined my son, Cassandra, without me he might not survive and god help you if he does not."

"The sun!" she yells again, anxious and angry. "You don't have the time Richard, you will never make it." He looks to the sky and then to his watch. Anger and fear explode across his face as he looks down the road, hoping his son will be ok, hoping he could hold on until he reaches him, maybe tonight.

Chapter 4

I opened my eyes slowly, not knowing where I was. The light immediately blinded me. I kept my eyes low to protect them from the sun beaming and burning my retinas. All I could remember from last night was the horrid screams of the lurker, then, in my memory, there was nothing, just darkness. I had no idea where I was or what had happened after. Staring down, the burning in my eyes subsided and the white spots dissipated. I realised I was still in the back of the car. It took me a moment to recognise these unfamiliar back seats. My head throbbed. My back still ached from the lurker throwing me from the driver's seat. My chest felt heavy like someone was pushing down on it. I raised my head, squinting, to see Kimmy's head lying on my chest, asleep. I thanked God right there and then that she managed to get us both out of there alive. I knew how scared she must had been while watching this monster feed on me and seeing how helpless I was against it. And yet, she managed. Somehow, we both were alive and safe in the back of the estate.

I raised my right arm slightly and a pain shot down from my shoulder where she had bitten me. The image and growls came flying back into the foremost of my thoughts. I tried not to make a noise as I wanted Kimmy to rest a little longer. I did not know how long she had been driving for after the attack and, regardless, she would need her sleep from all the events of last night.

With my left hand, I lightly stroked her hair, trying not to wake her but finding comfort in her presence and touch.

"Morning," she said, brightly. I jumped and she nearly fell off the seat with me.

"God, Kimmy, I thought you were asleep," I said gathering myself together after the shock.

She let out a little giggle. "How you feeling?"

She placed her chin on my chest, looking directly at me and seeing her big blue eyes made me feel ten times better already, so I did not lie when I replied, "I feel good. I'm sorry you had to get us out of there by yourself."

"Hey, hey, don't stress about that. We're alright."

"What happened? Where are we?" She did not answer immediately but first leaned over and kissed me on the lips gently. It felt so nice to just lie here and be able to relax with Kimmy without having to drive or keep an eye out. That's the beauty of the day: lurkers cannot come out in the sun. And for some reason, the sun was extra bright today.

She put her head back down on my chest and muttered, "I drove until the sun came up. I don't know where we are. As soon as I could, I bandaged up your back as you were bleeding all over."

At that, I realised that I had a white bandage across my chest, wrapping my back up. I could not believe that she had managed all this whilst in such a scary situation. I couldn't help myself and kissed her.

“You are amazing, you know that?”

She smiled at me and pressed her head into my chest. It hurt my back a little bit but I held back the pain as I didn't want her to see how hurt I was. I gave her a little nudge to let her know that I wanted to sit up. I needed to stretch so, slowly and agonizingly, I climbed out of the car, took a deep breath of fresh air and stretched my whole body. As I reached my arms up, I almost every inch of my body protested but the stretch itself felt amazing, despite the pain.

As I stretched and the ache from sleeping squashed in the back seats lifted, I took a good look around. I gazed at the fields and rolling hills on either side of us. There was not another car in sight. The sun was beaming across a pure blue sky, it was such a nice day. If we were in any other situation, I would have been wanting to go for a nice picnic with Kimmy and invite other friends along, in one of the parks near us in London.

I shouted to Kimmy to come out look at how nice the day was. After everything we had been through last night, we deserved a bit of peace and to enjoy this beautiful weather, maybe go take a good lie down on the grass for a while and just relax. After all, we were going to make it to Castleford within a few more hours and the sun would still be shining when we arrived. Now it was daylight, we had no rush to get there.

I turned back around to the car to coax Kimmy out as she had not yet joined me but as I did, yet again, I turned to find there was a gun pointed right in my face. This time, it was held by a man with scruffy brown hair and a face smudged in dirt as if he had been sleeping in a ditch. He looked about forty or so and had a double-barrelled shotgun. I took this in matter-of-factly, perhaps getting used to being threatened with firearms. I looked towards the car and there was a younger man, with similar features and so probably his son, pulling Kimmy out of the car. He was armed too with a handgun of some kind. He was not being rough with her, just pulling her out of the car. I looked back to the man pointing a gun in my face.

They didn't look like killers or even bad people for that matter; he looked more scared than me. Humans in the bright sunshine, armed or not, were certainly less scary than the three lurkers we had encountered last night.

"What do you want, mister?" I asked him calmly. He stepped back a few steps and shouted "Come on" to a woman with long brown hair and a raggedy dress who came towards the car holding a young boy, no older than 10. She stood on the other side of the car near the passenger's seat.

Kimmy looked at me. "Stuart?" she says, the hurt apparent in her eyes.

"Just don't move, babe, do as he says."

He signalled to her to move away from the car and then said to me, "We're taking the car, lad. We don't want any trouble, just don't move and nobody gets hurt."

They were just a scared family, clearly hiding out in the fields, terrified that lurkers could find them at any time, each night, and now they had the chance to get somewhere safe faster with our car. But, of course, if they took our car, Kimmy and I would be stranded in the middle of nowhere and who knew how far away the next safe place could be. The man started to move towards the car, stepping backwards and keeping his gun and eyes on me.

"Sir, don't do this. We can travel all together. There's room if we all squeeze."

The young man forced Kimmy to the back of the car by aggressively but clumsily pointing the gun at her, playing at being a soldier. Then he made his way round to the driver's seat and paused before jumping in. "Dad," he shouted, "let's go!"

"If you leave us here, we could die," I said slowly to the man. I could see the regret in his face, but he went to walk away.

"Sir, please! If you leave us here, we could die," I begged, far more emphatically this time.

He stared at me as he gathered his thoughts, "I can't. I have to think about my family first. I'm sorry, lad."

The boy shouted again, "Dad, come on!"

Using the distraction as the man looked at his son, I reacted, reaching out as fast as I could, knocking the shotgun out of his hands and catching it. I then pointed it back at him.

The boy shouted again, "hey", while grabbing his own gun from where he had thrown it on the dashboard. He was pointing it at me.

"Lower your gun," I ordered.

He trembled but kept his voice steady, "No. You lower yours."

"Kimmy, come here," I said but then he pointed the gun at her instead.

"Hey" I shouted and aimed the shotgun right into his father's face. "You keep that gun on me.

He obeyed. I could see the fear in the young lad's face but I was scared too, scared that if they left us out here my girlfriend and I would become meals to lurkers. I could not risk our lives for some strangers, especially given this stunt they were pulling. They had not even considered co-operating. These were the first other humans we had seen in nearly a year. God save us if this was what our country had become.

Kimmy slowly moved behind me, into safety. “I can’t let you take our car,” I said. The lad looked to his father, who stood there with his hands up in surrender. The lad glanced at me and then I heard the little boy stood there with his mother say, Daddy quietly. I was so angry at them for trying to take what little we had and leave us stranded. And yet, I could also feel my eyes watering because they had a little boy more helpless then any of us. The man shouted to his little boy, “It’s okay, Dillon, you just stay over there, daddy's gonna be fine.”

Somehow, I was now the bad guy. I felt like the one in the wrong even though they were the ones stealing our car. But it was not really our car, was it? And the cabin hadn’t been ours and the world was utterly messed up.

Kimmy placed her hands on my shoulders, comfortingly, and gently whispered, “Let them go, Stuart,”

“But we’ll be stranded here,” I replied, pained.

“I know, but they have a child, and we can find another way.”

I felt my eyes warm and a stream of tears rolled out from them and down my cheeks.

“We don’t know how far away anything is.”

I knew I had to lower the gun but as soon as I did the car would be gone along with our supplies and Kimmy and I were stranded out in the middle of nowhere. I didn't want to risk any harm coming to Kimmy but if I were to take the car back, the little boy and the whole family would be then be stranded and I knew I would regret that for the rest of my life, unsure whether I sentenced them to death. At least if I let them go, the father would have to deal with that guilt and at least I could be comforted knowing I had helped them survive.

"Stuart," Kimmy whimpers in my ear, pleading.

I lowered the gun slowly and he drew back as slowly, grabbing his elder son's shoulders as he did, walking backwards towards the car. Kimmy held me tight as they backed away, letting me know without words that I had done the right thing. The man looked back after his eldest son was safely in the back seat and thanked us from that distance before jumping into the driver's seat and driving away.

Kimmy and I sat down in the middle of the road and just watched them drive off until they were a speck on the horizon.

I felt like breaking down. Enjoying a beautiful day for few minutes had ruined our chances of survival. Even during the day when we were supposed to be safe from danger, we had still been robbed and threatened. This world was dark and cruel with humans turning against each other too and I wanted things to return to before. I turned around and wrapped my arms around Kimmy who had been much more mature about this than me.

She whispered in my ear, "We're going to be fine, Stuart."

I should be the one comforting her, but then again, she had always been stronger than I gave her credit for. I let out a big sigh.

"I know, babe, I'm just frustrated that's all. We could have been at your parents' within a few hours, and now we're stuck."

I tried to be optimistic. We still had possibilities after all. This would not be a death sentence unless we gave up. There must be a junction somewhere down this road, within walking distance, and, hopefully, there will be another working car that we could jack and we might be straight back on our way to Castleford. I held the shotgun in my left hand, took Kimmy's hand with my right, gave her a little reassuring smile and we set off walking up the road.

We walked for around an hour before we finally came up to a junction signposted 'Welcome to Rotherham'. Seeing that, we both finally knew exactly where we were - we had reached Yorkshire. I should have noticed the man and his son's accents but I guess no one thinks about accents when someone is stealing their car while pointing a gun at them. I took Kimmy by the arm and we started jogging into the town. The sun was still up but it was much closer to the horizon than I would have liked. Soon it would be dark. We needed to find a car quickly and get back on the road before night fell. Rotherham is only a small town compared to likes of london or leeds so it should not be hard to find something even if we were not expecting to find keys in the ignition. We ran over a round about and down the road that leads into town. We could see all the buildings just down the road but everywhere looked empty. Walking had been fine but this final exertion seemed too much for my shoulder which started to hurt and made me sweat. I carried on for a hundred more yards but then had to stop, panting as my shoulder throbbed with a stabbing pain, a pain so bad I fell to my knees. Kimmy grabbed me shouting my name and asking me what was wrong but it was too painful for me to answer. I had to scream and to release the pain that was shooting through my body. I felt like multiple knives were stabbing me on my shoulder in quick succession. For not the first time in the last twenty-four hours, I thought I was dying. And then the pain just suddenly stopped. My heart was pounding so hard that it felt like it was trying to break through my ribs, my breathing was as heavy as if the wind had been knocked out of my lungs. I had to sit for a bit and rest while I caught my breath.

"Are you ok, Stuart? Stuart?" Kimmy was still asking me, incessantly. I had to reply as soon as I was able. I could see how confused and scared she was.

“Yeah, I'm fine now, just my shoulder, I don’t know what happened. It just started hurting.”

Kimmy moved my shirt collar out of the way and lifted up the bandage to check. She recoiled and I could tell that there was something wrong. Her face was terrified. I was apprehensive, not wanting to look but I had too so I turned my head slowly, pulling my shoulder forward to see where the lurker had bitten me. The bite had turned green and black and had spread across my shoulder, infected. It looked repulsive. I covered it back up, manoeuvring the bandage so my shirt would not rub on it and raised my collar. I stood up, ready to set off again now the pain had subsided. Kimmy had her face in her hands. Her mother was a nurse, so she knew far more about infection than most people, but even I knew that this one was not going to be a walk in the park. I took her hands gently and lifted them from her face and held them comforting her.

“I'm gonna be fine, Kimmy. All we have to do is make it to your parents then your mum will know what to do.”

She nodded in agreement and wiped away the tears that streamed down her cheeks.

“We need to find a car. We can’t just sit here,” she said, pulling herself up. I was so proud of her taking control like that and pushing herself to keep moving on. She had become so much stronger as the weeks passed. Those first few weeks after the bombs hit, she had been a nervous wreck. I had not thought it possible that she could be as in control of her emotions as she was proving herself now to be.

She took my hand and we started a gentle jog down towards the town centre.

Rotherham was like a ghost town. Things had changed drastically since the last time we had driven through, visiting her parents after our last semester of university. I could not hear a thing. It was so eerily quiet for late afternoon. All the shops were empty, their windows smashed and their interiors empty. None had anything left in them. This was probably a reaction to the bombing: it made sense that people would have lost control and looted, trying to claim as many supplies as they could to support their own families. As with the family who took our car, it looked like people had been fending for themselves instead of working together. Could I blame them? We had, in our own way, done the same, hiding in the woods, playing house and ignoring the world outside.

The silence was broken. As we passed more building, very quietly I could hear something. It was definitely people talking amongst themselves, a sound I had not heard in so many months. I reacted quickly, pushing Kimmy up against the wall which shocked her so I put my finger to her lips to signal to her to not make a noise. I tried to listen again but I could not make out any words. It sounded like they were just around the corner, so I left Kimmy where she was and sidled along the wall to take a quick look around. The sun had not yet set so they must be other humans but, after today's experiences, I was suspicious of everyone. If everyone was fending for themselves, humans could also be dangerous and it was not a risk I was willing to take.

I took a quick glimpse around the corner but there was nothing there other than rubbish flowing across the street. I could hear the people though, as if they were right there. Where were they then? I could hear the unmistakable deepness of a man's voice and a higher voice replying to him, perhaps a young boy or a woman. I returned to Kimmy, took her by the arm and, together, we slowly crept around the corner. I realised that the sun was going down so we did not have much time to find a quiet street and a car, but with these people close by we could not risk running out into the open. We came up to a smashed window of a shop and I thought that they must be in there. I took a slow look round the corner into the shop, and suddenly I got this small migraine behind my eyes and my ears began to hurt as well and the speaking stopped abruptly. I pushed myself up against the wall and the head pain vanished immediately.

I could feel Kimmy shaking as she tried to control her breathing but I could still hear the tremor in each breath. We had to find shelter quickly as it was sunset now. I took her hand as I realised we had to risk it. Cautious of the pain in my back and head which could come back if I strained myself, we ran as silently as possible to end of the block and stopped at the corner. I peered around that corner but there was no car on that side. I looked down the other way and each was empty. There were no cars to be seen anywhere. We were going to have to find somewhere to hide, but where would be safe? Any of these buildings could have lurkers in them.

Kimmy squeezed my hand tighter as she signalled towards the sun, aware of the danger we were in.

I had no concrete plan, we were just going to have to hope for the best, take a guess and pick a building to hide in. At least, I had the shotgun to defend us, which made me feel a little safer.

There was a corner shop across the road. I signaled to Kimmy that we should aim for that one. I whispered to her to be fast and quiet which probably did not need saying. She looked at me and nodded but as she did, we heard a smash. It came from the corner we had just looked around. I peered around it again and saw a man staring at me from the second floor of a building opposite, then he jumped in through that window he had smashed.

I gestured at Kimmy to start running now. We set off in unison. She squeezed my hand tighter and the familiar pressure of it kept me calm while it comforted her as we ran across the road and up to the door of the corner shop. I pulled it open and the bells attached to the door to tell the shopkeeper they have a customer jingled loudly.

"Fuck" was all I could muster. Both Kimmy's and my eyes shot to the window where the man had been. We stared at the surrounding street for what felt like ages hoping that he had not heared the bells. It was silent and, as always when I was trying to listen for danger, the wind blew gently. The door made the slightest creak as I gently lent on it to open it further, but before I knew what was happening, the man had grabbed the gun out of my hand and hit me round the head with it. I skid across the floor and my vision blurred so that I could barely see anything. Surprisingly, I could not hear Kimmy screaming and the absence made me panic and forced me to stand while trying to make out where they were through the blur. My vision started to return to normal and I could see him strangling Kimmy up against the window of the corner shop. She was looking right at me, while ineffectually trying to bat him off, her eyes bulging and her face shining red from the pressure of his hands around her throat. I knew that I probably would not even budge him but I had to do something seeing Kimmy staring at me unable to breathe. The fear spread across her face sent this rush of anger through my body, and I threw myself into his back, tackling him and, miraculously, he went skidding across the floor I was nonplussed, staring at him on the floor, wondering how I managed that when I had heard that it is physically impossible for a human to overpower a lurker, but the severity of the situation came flooding back and I wasted no more time dwelling on it, lifted Kimmy from where she was choking on the floor.

"You okay?" She nodded holding her throat as she tried to catch her breath and we ran in the opposite direction to the lurker, both with ragged breath. We did not get far before he had grabbed me and pinned me up against the solid wall. He quickly went to bite me but my reflexes were taut and I grabbed his throat first, holding him off, but I could feel his strength over powering me as his fangs inched closer. I pushed with all the force I had, not understanding how I had even managed to last this long against a lurker. All of a sudden, Kimmy broke a brick over the lurker's head. She did not have the strength to floor him but he did hesitate and it gave me time to push him off me. I ran towards Kimmy and stood in front of her, protectively. There was no way that we were going to out run this monster and I had already dropped the gun. The only thing left to do was to fight him. He stared at me with confusion written across his face, his shining eyes scanning my body as he growled readying himself to attack exactly as the female lurker had last night before she bit me. My whole body was tense. I clenched my fists ready for what was coming. For the fourth time in twenty-four hours, we faced certain death at the hands of a single lurker. We could not possibly survive again but then again, this couldn't be it, not after what we had been through. I was not going to allow this beast to kill us both now. Maybe I could distract it long enough for Kimmy to run away and hide. He attacked, I yelled to her to run but as I did, a loud bang echoed through the streets, and now the lurker was screaming on the floor, making a noise so horrible that it sent shivers through my whole body. Confused, I left him screaming on the floor, and began scanning the area to see whether our saviour was our friend or foe. At first, I saw no one but then a woman with brown hair to her shoulders who looked to be in her thirties and wearing a black leather jacket and combat jeans came walking out of a house over the road from where we were. She walked past me and right up to the lurker who was still screaming on the floor and, without a second's hesitation, she put another bullet straight through his head.

She completely ignores Kimmy and I and shouts past us, "He's down!"

I looked around to see who she was talking to, assumedly the man coming out of another house from the other side of the street, a similar age to the woman.

He had short blonde hair and a long duffel jacket and was confidently holding a handgun loosely in his right hand.

"Wooo, nice shot, Mes!" he shouted as he walked up to her and gave her a fist bump. He looked at us and then pointed the gun straight at me. "You, who are ya?" he asked in a friendly manner, despite the treat of the gun.

I did not want to give them any reason to be angry with us if they were taking out lurkers so easily so I answered quickly, "My name is Stuart and this is my girlfriend Kimmy."

Kimmy squeezed my hand, still very much shaken by yet another attack. Her hands shook so I gave her a small squeeze back. I did not know what it was about these two but I wasn't scared of this man, even though he was pointing a gun at me. For some reason, I had a good feeling about them and instinctively knew that we weren't in danger. He put the gun in his jacket and walked up to me.

"Well Stuart, Kimmy, I'm Alex and this crazy little bitch is my sister, Mes."

She put her rifle over her shoulder. "Short for Mary," she says.

The man put his hand out to shake mine but I hesitated, despite my instinct to trust him. "It's a hand mate, you're supposed to shake it when you meet someone new," he teases me with a grin on his face. I smirked back.

"Yeah, I know sorry," I replied laughing, "it's just been a long time since I've had to do it, that's all."

I put my hand out and took his in a firm grip and shook it. Mes did the same to Kimmy and then we switched. Kimmy looked at me as we did and I could see her relax - we instinctively knew that we weren't in danger with these two.

"Welcome to the Rotherham camp, guys," Alex said to us.

Not knowing what he meant by 'the camp', I just replied with a confused, "What?" knowing that I was not being as cool as I wanted but too tired and confused to try harder.

"The Rotherham camp, mate, where you have found yourselves. Come on, let's get you both inside before anything else shows up. That screamer made a fair bit of noise, we don't want any more unwanted company."

They set off down the road and Kimmy and I followed them, hand in hand.

Chapter 5

We walked down a few blocks and I wondered whether this was the man and woman I heard talking before. Were they watching us, waiting and following us while we were trying to find a safe place? If they were, why come to our rescue at the last minute? Why would they not help us earlier when the sun was still up. They must have seen us, because I heard them talking as if they were right next to us, but when I looked, they were nowhere to be seen. I started getting suspicious again. Maybe this was a game to the two of them, maybe they were using us as bait for the lurker. But then again, I could not tell whether the voices were theirs. Mes' may well have been too low for the woman or boy

I heard. I could not remember distinctly enough.

Using us for bait or not, I could tell they had been doing whatever this was for a while, hiding out in this town, looking out for each other, just the two of them, learning how to be invisible and fight back against the lurkers.

Alex stopped us in front of a building with a big grey shutter. I wanted to ask why have we stopped here? But before I could get a word out Alex looked too us both.

"Welcome to the base friends."

He banged on the shutter three times paused and then banged twice more. I followed the sounds that came from within. I could hear a door unlocking very clearly, then a padlock being opened, then the shutter started to slide open to reveal a black woman stood in the entrance as it lifted. She had close-cropped thick black hair and a green tank top with black combat trousers on. As she saw us, her smile faded and she frowned.

"Who are these two?" she asked with an accent merged between african and english. She did not sound too happy about us being there. I might even describe her tone as slightly aggressive.

"These Tina, are our new friends, Stuart and Kimmy."

Her expression did not change. "Why did you bring them here, Alex?" she snarled at him.

"Oh calm down, ya miserable git and let us in," said Mes quickly, barging past her into the building. Alex signalled for the two of us to follow but as we went to walk past Tina, she continued to glare at Kimmy and I as if we were the enemy. I tried smiling at her but to no avail and I could tell she was making Kimmy uncomfortable. I also felt very unwelcome given her reaction to us two.

We didn't want an enemy and what if the others were equally as hostile. We carried on into the building anyway, following Alex and Mes. Tina locked up behind us and brought up the rear.

The place was far bigger on the inside than we had any reason to believe from the outside. Walls had been knocked down through each building either side of this one creating a vast warehouse-like space. All the windows and doors were welded shut with metal girders and steel slabs. I couldn't believe what I was seeing as we walked through the base as they called it. I understood now why Alex had called it a camp. People were talking together, kids ran around, chasing each other, having fun. Everyone stopped as we entered their space to look at us, but newcomers must not have been that uncommon because most people just smiled and carried on as they were. There must have been dozens of people there, living together, like a refuge of survivors creating their own community.

Kimmy's expression mirrored my own as she could not believe her own eyes at what we were seeing. Tears were building up in her eyes as I felt my own get wet. Alex noticed and took us by our shoulders.

"It's something, ain't it?" he said, staring down through the base with a sense of pride and a smile that lit up his face.

"How have you done this? How long have you been here living like this?" Kimmy asked. She was barely able to get her words out.

"What are you talking about? We are part of the rebellion, like I said, this is the Rotherham camp." As he said this, he could tell we had no idea what he was talking about because we looked at each other dumbfounded. These were the first people we had seen in months, apart from the family that stolen our car and the lurkers that had tried to kill us within the last day. We had seen no other soul since the bombs dropped.

"How do you not know about the rebellion?" he asked, slowly. "How is that possible? We have been fighting back since the bombs went off. There are camps all over the country, in most cities and towns. How have you not come across another over all these months?"

I could not believe what I was hearing. While Kimmy and I had been hiding out in the woods, assuming that almost everyone had been killed, there had been survivors living, and not only that, they were working together and fighting back. The hope I had lost when the family stole our car came back in full force. As horrible as the world now was, here was safety and a group of humans who were united and helped each other.

"We really haven't been in touch with anybody since the bombs went off. We had no idea what was going on in the outside world."

He gave us both a surprised look but he quickly took control of the situation. "Well you've got a lot to learn then. Come with me." He ushered us further through the base until we reached a room off the main area. Mes was already in there talking to a huge man, scarred down his left cheek. This scar ran right up into his grey hair and down his neck to where it was hidden by the collar of his camo army jacket. He scared me. He had a formidable presence. They stopped talking as we entered. Tina was sat down in a chair in the corner and she ignored us rather than continuing with her open hostility. The room was small which made the man look even bigger. There were names written on the wall under which were pictures of men, women, children, and next to that was an old black board, straight from a school in the 90's, marked up in chalk with plans of some sort covering it. There was a table in the middle of the room and Mes and the man were stood either side of it.

"So, these are the two drifters then?" the big man said. Alex stepped forward.

"Yep, John meet Stuart and Kimmy. We found them trying to fight off a lurker; we saved them just in time."

Mes cleared her throat and Alex cast a little smile back to her.

"Well, more accurately, Mes saved them."

"Which camp have you travelled from? " John turned to us and asked, brusquely.

Alex jumped in again before I could do more than open my mouth to respond.

"Actually, John, they don't come from any camp."

"What?" the three of them said almost in unison, confusion and surprise splashing across every stoic face.

"They didn't even know about the rebellion, mate."

John grabbed a cup off the table and walked up to the two of us still in the doorway. I steadily and nervously slid Kimmy behind me. I wasn't sure how this man was going to react to us. Mes seemed indifferent and Tina was clearly not happy about us being there so why would this man accept us? And it was clear he was the one in charge here.

He took a long sip of the drink he was holding while keeping his eyes sternly on us both, then asked, "Where you come from then?"

I quickly answered, "We were living in London, but we've been living in a cabin in the woods near Luton since the bombs dropped. You are all the first people we've had contact with since then."

"The woods?" Alex laughed. "I'm surprised you lasted this long."

John continued to give us a long hard look. "Get them a room," he eventually tells Mes. Then he turned back to us. "You must be tired. Get some rest. We will fill you in on everything in the morning but now, it's night which is no time for messing around with newcomers. It's your decision what you do in the morning. Until then, welcome to the Rotherham camp."

We were clearly dismissed and followed Mes dutifully to a room a few doors down. "Ya can sleep here for the night. Don't worry about John, he's old-fashioned army, was in the military for decades. He likes to be intimidating but he's like a big dad to everyone around here. He looks after us all, treats this like a military base, it works though. We're all still breathing and that's what matters, right?"

She did not seem to want an answer and did not wait for one. She gave us a friendly nod each and walked off. I looked further down the hall and saw a woman there cradling a new-born baby in her arms. She looked up and gave me the warmest smile. Everybody else was quietly going into their rooms with their families, friends, partners. I couldn't believe how calm and natural they all were in the middle of a town at night. The lurkers could be on the other side of the wall but these people all looked like there was nothing to fear.

Kimmy took my arm softly and pulled me into the room, there was a single bed in the corner with a couple of rags thrown over it. It didn't look very comfortable but considering our situation there was no complaining. It would be far better than a kerb or a ditch out in the dark with no protection.

Kimmy jumped onto the bed, sprawling as she let out a huge sigh of relaxation.

"Can you believe this, Stuart? This place!" she exclaimed as she reached for me and pulled me onto the bed and I had to take back my internal remark expecting it to be uncomfortable. I lay on my back and just sank into the mattress, feeling my body making its own depression in it as if it was brand new. Taking the weight off of my feet been able to relax, it felt like I hadn't laid in a bed for years.

"Would you ever have believed that there would have been a place like this?" Kimmy whispered softly to me.

"Not at all, babe."

"Did you see all the kids playing and the woman with the baby. They all looked so safe and content," she went on a little rant about what she had seen, happier than I had seen her in a while.

"Yeah I know. It's amazing, hun." She rolled herself on top of me into a position where she was sitting on my stomach. I could see the excitement in her face.

"You know what this means, right?" she asked.

"What?" I was enjoying the feel of the mattress and her weight on top of me and had no brain power to work out what she could be referring to.

"What if my family are at a camp. They could even be at this camp. We're not that far from Castleford, really. They could easily have made their way here." She suddenly leapt up with excitement and walked towards the door.

"Babe stop, what ya doing?"

"I'm off to go check if they're here."

I jumped up and gently took Kimmy's hand.

"Babe, I don't think that's a good idea. We don't know anybody here. They told us to go to bed and they could get nervous about us looking around and interrupting their evenings. Everyone went to their rooms after all. I mean that Tina didn't react very well to us, and John, well I'm not sure about him, he wanted to get us away from him pretty fast it seemed. Let's wait until tomorrow. Alex will know who is here and not, probably, and if not, John will. We can ask them in the morning."

I gently placed my hands behind her head and brought our foreheads together. She stared into my eyes and the lamplight from the room glimmered in her big blue eyes. I watched as she took a time to think about it, then she replied, "yeah you're right."

A quiet knock at the door made us both jump. I stood up and placed myself where I would block Kimmy from danger as the door crept open slowly. I did not know what to expect but I was jumpy and wary after all our experiences over the last two days. I wasn't going to believe that we were safe anywhere until I was totally sure. The last time I had let my guard down, the family stolen our car after all. I believed humans would do anything to survive even if it meant killing other humans.

As the door fully opened, there was a little girl stood in the doorway. She had long blonde hair and was dress in dungarees over a white jumper and she was holding a basket. She looked about seven years old and she looked up at us with the most innocent look I had ever seen. As wary as I was, I was never going to be suspicious of this small angelic-looking child.

"Hi," she said softly and her voice was as gentle and innocent as her appearance.

Kimmy walked straight up to her and knelt down in front of her, "Hi, what's your name, then?" she asked the little girl.

"Sarah", she replied.

"Hi Sarah, I'm Kimmy."

I remembered when we used to talk about having a family, Kimmy always wanted a little girl. I would protest and say, "nope, we're having a boy", but I knew that didn't really matter what we had, Kimmy would be an amazing mother. She is so caring and loving. I couldn't think of any one better to raise a child. Never having a real mother or father, I don't know how I would be, but I knew I would try my best and that I would never leave my family like my parents did me - I couldn't bring that life upon a child.

"I brought you some food," the girl said.

She handed the basket to Kimmy, "Well thank you very much! Aren't you just the most generous and beautiful little girl in the world?"

The little girl smiled. "Thank you," she said dutifully and ran off.

Kimmy closed the door after her and then turned around with the biggest of smiles spread across her face. "Oh my god, she was so adorable."

She put down the basket and hugged me with her head on my chest in her favourite position to cuddle in. At that point, I thought I knew what she was about to say and I was not disappointed:

"I want one." She looked up at me and I kissed her on the lips and squeezed her tighter. I couldn't bring a child in to the world right now and I knew that Kimmy knew that, the child had made her broody. There was no point in dashing her dreams now, all I could say was the truth about what I wanted. "One day babe, we will."

She looked at me with wide eyes, "Really?"

"Of course, I couldn't think of anything better than starting a family with you. I love you and I know that you would be a brilliant mother."

At that point, she leaned forward and kissed me softly while moving her hands up my next and into hair. Before I knew it, she had adroitly clambered on top of me with her legs straddling my chest. I stroked her body, letting my hands enjoy the feel of her soft skin, rubbing gently and made my way down to her bottom then slowly back up to her body. The blood rushed around my body as my heartbeat sped up. Kimmy started to unbutton my shirt as she stared intensely into my eyes. She left it unbuttoned and around my arms and her hands slid under the material, gripping my chest, grazing every muscle. My hands ran down to the back of her thighs and I dexterously scooped her up from my chest and laid her down gently and lovingly onto the bed, kissing her neck as she ran her hands up my arms and moved to my back.

I paused kissing her neck so she could pull her top off over her head, revealing her petite body. I caressed the lower part of her stomach with my lips, then slowly up towards her breasts, fumbling to take off her bra at the same time. When I had, I ran my tongue around her breasts and she gasped as my tongue grazed her nipple. We were both breathing heavily, feeling more and more connected with every passionate touch. I unbuttoned her jeans, sliding them off gently. She sat up quickly and gripped my belt too, loosening it and it was her turn to run her lips over my chest while she unbuttoned my jeans and she slowly pulled them down. I laid back down on top of her, kissing her harder and locking tongues. I used my left arm to pull down her knickers as she dragged mine down to my ankles ferociously. I wrapped her hair around my fingers to pull her head back, licking and kissing her neck. She rubbed her hands down my back, squeezing it tighter every time I pulled at her hair. Our bodies entwined moving together hotter and faster. I placed my lower body between her thighs and thrust hard and she clawed at my back almost tearing my skin as we meet and her head is thrown back. , I couldn't help but thrust harder, forcing her to moan in pleasure and scratch at my back even harder. I pulled her hair tighter and felt my way down to her left thigh and wrenching it higher as she wrapped her legs around my lower back. I squeezed her legs and thrust faster and harder. Our bodies rubbed together, blood rushing, slick with sweat, hearts beating together harder and faster. I strengthened my position on top of her but she rolled us over and forced herself on top. My hands ran up and down her back as she rode her body back and forth in perfect motion. My hands cupped and squeezed her bottom then ran up to her breasts. She pushed her breasts to my chest and ran her hands through my hair, covering me in kisses as she gasped and our hot breath flowed over each other. She stopped kissing me and as she stared into my eyes, I could tell that the feeling was getting stronger for both of us as our bodies got tighter and tighter, reacting to each other's motions. I could feel my own climax increasing with every thrust, and her moans got louder, her grip tightened. I rolled back on top of her, my hand taking her hair again, thrusting harder biting gently. Her legs began to judder, her moans got louder, my blood rushed harder, then the feeling of release flowed through my body as I couldn't hold it in any longer. She squeezed my back one last time and moaned as she too released. I began to slow down; my heart was pounding so hard I could hear it throbbing in my ears. Our bodies were drenched in sweat. My muscles started to relax again. I loosened my grip from her hair as I came out, slowly moving my lips from her neck to her lips gently kissing while trying to catch our breath. Our lingering gaze was full of love, trust and pure happiness.

My head rested on her chest as we both caught our breath. I could feel her heart beating so loudly it was as if it was trying to reach out to me from inside her body.

She stroked my hair gently and I slid myself up to lie properly on the bed next to her. She cuddled in, partly across my chest to fit in the cramped single bed. I pulled the rags over us and she wrapped her arm across my front. I ran my fingers up and down her arm as I normally do when she is upset to ground her and let her know I'm here. I loved doing it because she loved it, no matter her mood. I was rewarded as I felt her heartbeat calm down and her breathing return to normal.

We lay like that for a while, quietly, happy in the comfort of each other's arms. Then the noise of Kimmy's sweet snore began to vibrate from her as she drifted off into a much-needed sleep. My eyelids were getting heavier by the second so I closed them. Then all of a sudden, without conscious movement, I was stood up next to the bed. I turned to my left and a man was right there, standing smiling back at me but I could not see his face, just his fangs shining out from that twisted smile. It sent a shiver radiating through my whole body. Then my heart went cold as I realised that he had Kimmy in his arms. Shock ran through me like an explosion as, without hesitation, he tore into her throat. I ran to help as fast as I possibly could but I still was not close enough and couldn't get to her in time. He threw her to the floor, finished with her. I hurt so much from regret and losing her it was agonising as I looked down to her lifeless body. I could not save her. The man turned his gaze back to me. I was struck by fear with what I saw and I could not fully comprehend it: the man who killed Kimmy, who tore into my true love's throat like she was nothing but a piece of meat to be eaten, was me. Suddenly, he grabbed me by the face and stared into my eyes as if he was looking straight into my soul.

"This is what you are," he said, in a sadistically dark voice, nothing like my own, and the next thing I knew I could hear Kimmy.

"Stuart, STUART! Wake up!" She got louder, almost screaming at me "WAKE UP, STUART!" I regained consciousness properly and realised I was still in bed thrashing about, held down.

“Stop Stuart, it’s me look, look!” She took my head with her hands and pulled my face towards hers. I was conscious now and could see that it really was Kimmy and I immediately stopped thrashing around. My blood was boiling, almost painful enough for me to scream out in agony. My head was splitting like it had been hit with a sledge hammer. I almost jumped up out of bed screaming from the feeling of anger over seeing her dead body. I gazed back into Kimmy's eyes as she wrestled me to the mattress. Red blurs took over my vision as if blood was covering my eyes, but I tried to concentrate on her eyes, her beautiful, bright, confused, scared eyes. I started to breathe, to try and take control of my own body. The fear in her face pushed me to fight whatever this attack was.

She began stroking my hair, whispering gently into my ear, “It’s fine, babe, it’s fine, babe, I'm here,” as she cradled me like a baby.

The infection from my shoulder wound must be playing with my mind as it slowly killed my body. I could feel it as soon as I woke up, the infection was getting worse and without medication it wouldn't be long until it would be too late. Kimmy must have had the same thought because she held me so tightly that I could hear the slight shiver in her breathing and then she laid me back down on the bed and suggested, hesitantly, “Let’s take another look at your shoulder.”

She turned me over and pulled my shirt down at the back, past my shoulder. Her hands shot to her mouth. I could not bear to look myself after her reaction, the very sight must be horrific, but I forced myself to look.

There was nothing there. I was shocked and bewildered. I grabbed my shoulder with my hand, pulling it forward as my neck craned further around to see lower but there was nothing there. Not even a scratch, let alone the bite marks, the discolouration and the bruising from earlier. I jumped out of bed and pulled my shirt off.

“Look.” I turned my back to Kimmy. “Is there anything there?” I felt it as she slowly ran her hands up my back.

“No, nothing. It’s all healed, it’s gone. Stuart, how is this possible?”

I turned around and took Kimmy's hands. She seemed half scared, half relieved. I did not know what to think let alone what to say to her. How could it be healed already? Even the bite wound was on my back gone. The infection could maybe have healed on its own which would be miraculous but just about possible. But the puncture marks drew blood. There was nothing even indicating where they had been. It happened less than twenty-four hours ago. How could it have healed already. But before we could say anything else, Alex barged through the door.

“Keep quiet, get ready and come with me, quickly,” he ordered from the doorway, not looking at us in our half-clothed state. He closed the door gently. We had a new problem now. Had John decided what to do with us already? I was not sure how long I had been asleep but I did not think that my nightmare lasted more than twenty minutes. Regardless, it certainly was not more than a couple of hours since we left them.

I placed my hands round Kimmy's terrified and confused face.

“Babe it’s gonna be okay. We will deal with this later, yeah?” She gave me a slight nod but I could see the worry in her eyes and they had started to well up.

“Hurry up, you two!” he whispered urgently but very quietly from the other side of the door. I quickly grabbed my clothes and frantically pulled my trousers on and buttoned up my shirt, scrambling over the buttons. Kimmy finished dressing and nervously tried to sort out her hair. I took her by the hand and crept out of the door nervously. Alex signalled us to keep quiet, his finger to his lips.

We tiptoed through the building until we came to a room. John, Mes, Tina and a few other people were already there, staring at a few screens on the far wall. They were all armed, strapped up with guns and ammo, looking like they were ready for war. No one paid the least attention to Alex, Kimmy and I entering, all their faces were pinned to these screens with a look that screamed trouble. This was clearly not about us then but I did not feel relief as whatever this was, it might well be much worse and their faces gave me no comfort.

We made our way into the room carefully to join the others as more people arrived. I could see the screens now too. They seemed to be linked to cameras outside because all I could see was dark empty streets and buildings with no lights on. I scanned through them all slowly then suddenly came to a stop as I saw a dark figure in the middle of the road on one screen. He looked as if he was staring right into the camera. I fastened my eyes to him and I had this sudden feeling that he could see me through the camera, that he was staring right at me, no one else, through the camera, The intensity of the moment grew, my heart began to beat louder and louder until all I could hear was the echoing thump vibrating through my body, beat after beat. He came more clearer as I looked through the camera myself, despite the darkness and poor image quality, a small man, brown hair.

The intensity grew as the seconds passed by. His face became clearer and clearer until I could see the bright brown flicker from his eyes. I couldn't look any more. The discomfort pulled my eyes away from the screen. I scanned the room and stopped at a digital clock on the table. It read 5:15am. It felt as if I had been asleep for only a few seconds but it had been hours.

If this man on the screen was a lurker, he would not be around for much longer.

It would not be long until the sun would be up, less than an hour probably.

I looked back to the screen and he was gone. I scanned all the other screens as fast as I could but he was nowhere to be seen.

“Right, listen up, soldiers” John said, breaking the uncomfortable silence which filled the room. “I’ve got a feeling that’s not the end of that. This beast saw the cameras, and I’m pretty sure he's going to come back to see who is operating them. As I see it, we have two choices. One, we can stay, hoping that he does not bring an army with him and if he comes back, we slay him ourselves or, two, we admit we have been compromised, pack up and move safely to the next camp.”

Everybody looked around, waiting for somebody to speak. Kimmy squeezed my hand tighter as tension in the room increased.

“Well don't all speak up at once,” John remarked.

I knew I didn't have any right to speak there. Considering how recently we had arrived, we shouldn’t have any say on the matters of the camp before we knew how it worked, especially not before we had even decided to stay.

Alex spoke up. “I say it’s not a big enough threat yet to spook everybody. Plus, it was only the one lurker. I would have gone out there myself and finished him if you’d let me.”

Mes jumped in immediately agreeing with her brother. “I’m with Alex. It was only one lurker, we didn't see any more on any of the cameras. We can take him. And with my experience, either lurkers are alone or they travel in packs. If there are more, they tend not to travel far from each other.”

I looked around the room to gauge everybody’s reaction and saw them generally nodding in agreement. John scanned the room too, looking for dissent.

“Does anybody have anything else to say, or do we agree with Alex and Mes?” he asked authoritatively. I was impressed. He seemed to have the authority of a tough leader who would do what was necessary but he was also clearly democratic, making sure everyone felt heard. He still scared me but I felt I could respect him.

The silence was profound. Then John looked directly at me, as if waiting for my response. He couldn't be wanting my opinion on the matter though. We didn't belong with this group; we were outsiders. But if I were to answer him, I would disagree. Everything in my body was telling me to get Kimmy out of there. I had a bad feeling that the lurker would come back and it would be trouble. I kept my face blank though and John moved on.

“Well then, everybody get some rest. Sun’s up soon. We’ll test our defences in the morning and we will need our energy to strengthen them before tomorrow night to ensure this camp is safe. I will not be losing anybody if this beast comes back, you hear me?” he said sternly.

“Yes sir,” they all replied obediently, like it was a military base and he were their captain, which, in a way, I guess it was.

Everyone filed out of the room and we began to follow, but I still could not help shake off this feeling that they were making the wrong decision, so I waited until everybody had gone, signalled to Kimmy to stay where she was for a moment, and returned to the room.

John was now sat at the table staring at the cameras with his feet on the desk crossed, drinking out of that same cup he had when we first met. The text was showing this time and I was surprised to see that it was a World’s Best Daddy mug. Another layer to him, I hadn’t thought of him as a family man but now assumed he must have a family here.

“You got summat to say?” he barked.

“I’m sorry I didn't speak up before but I didn't feel like it was my place to do so in front of everyone else.”

“What is it, then?”

“I think it’s a bad idea to stay. It’s too risky when we could just move on. What if he does come back with a group? As capable as your fighters are, these things are stronger and faster and there are children here to protect, sir.” I added the honorific to keep up respect as the other soldiers did.

“The decision has been made boy. You should have said earlier. You’re too late now,” he replied brusquely.

“But, sir-”

“But nothing,” he interrupted. “It’s made and that’s the end of it.” He was starting to get angry and that was the last thing I needed. I nodded, demurely and retreated, not wanting to get in an argument with this man. He was the real deal. He would batter me if it came to an argument and he commanded too much respect for me to try.

“The sun will be up soon. You heard me tell the others, get some rest, and if you feel like you need to leave, you and your girlfriend are free to go when the sun’s at its highest. But the decision is made. We are staying.”

I walked out in defeat. He wasn't going to change his mind now. He would follow the chosen plan until it was clear it would fail. He was set.

I put my arm around Kimmy and we walked back to the room to get some more rest. He was right. We were going to need it.

Chapter 6

Everything is pitch black, all I can hear is this buzzing sound. It sounds like a bee, just like a bee. It stops and starts intermittently. It is not regular enough to be electrical. It sounds just like a bee. It gets louder and louder unnaturally loud, until it sounds like the bee has landed in my ear. My eyes open slowly and my vision starts to clear. There is a bee but it is buzzing in the corner of the room then it stops and rests on the roof. It could not be further from me but it is so loud. I spread my arms to take hold of Kimmy but my arm feels nothing but a cold spot on the mattress where Kimmy should be. I jump up out of bed and throw my jeans and shirt back on. I hear noises from the other side of the door, but can't make out what I am hearing, then I hear a scream. Kimmy. I rush through the door, and there are people everywhere. No one looks the least perturbed. Where did the scream come from? What's going on? Did no one else hear it? I look to the left of me down the building and as I notice Kimmy, my heart begins to calm down, my panic lessens.

I zone in on her. Kimmy is sat on a chair in front of a bunch of children and she is reading a story to them. I can't quite make out the book from here but I think it might be Red Riding Hood. All the children are rapt, hanging onto every word she is saying. She smiles so broadly as she does the actions along with the dialogue. She looks so happy.

"Stuart." I hear someone say from my right and there's Alex stood at a table filling up gun magazines with one bullet at a time, like he is getting ready for battle.

“You alright, mate? Ya looking a little pale.”

I take another look at Kimmy. She is fine, I can leave her to enjoy her story with the children, so I head over to the table where Alex is.

“Yeah, thanks, I’m fine, just still coming to terms with everything.”

“What d’ya mean?”

“Well, we haven't really been around people for a long time, remember. It was just the two of us in a cabin in the woods for a full ten months before we left two nights ago. Getting back familiar with this much noise might take a little time.”

He lets out a little chuckle, “You decided to stay then?”

“I'm not sure yet, Alex, but look at her. I love seeing her like that. I wouldn't want to take her away from this if I don't have to”. What I am not saying is that I can't help but think about that lurker and the way he was looking through that camera. I’m sure he knew we were there and that he could see right through to me. I know he will be back.

“I understand your worry, mate. Ya scared for your girlfriend's safety, but you don’t know the camp. We’ve been fighting these things for a while now, and we have never had a breach in these halls. I believe where safe here, and we could always use someone like you to join us.”

He pauses and there is silent for a second. He looks at me as he rams the magazine into the rifle. “I saw how you handled yourself against that lurker to protect Kimmy. I’ve gotta say it really looked like you overpowered him for a second so you must be good at fighting them, but I’m not stupid, I know no human could overpower a lurker."

I think back to that moment and while I know that no human could overpower a lurker, I also am sure, for that split second when he was trying to bite me, my power grew and I did have the strength to throw him down. I knew it and the lurker felt it too. I saw the look on his face as he picked himself off the ground. The look expressed pure shock for what had just happened to him. I recognise that shock. It is how I still feel. How could I have been stronger than a lurker? And how could my wounds heal and why do I have sudden attacks of pain to my head? And why did everything seem slower, louder and a bit surreal?

"So, you ever fired one of these things?" Alex says, bringing me out of this whirlwind of thoughts.

"Yeah, I used to hunt rabbits back at the cabin."

"I think ya will have a bit of trouble trying to shoot a lurker, mate. They're a little bit faster than rabbits," he says but he has a cheeky smile on his face so I know he's only teasing me. "We'll hook you up with a rifle by tonight. I gotta go check the stocks."

He throws the rifles over his shoulder and goes to walk off. I remember that I was waiting to talk to him. "Alex, wait up a sec," I say. He pauses and turns back to me.

"What's up, mate?"

"You and John mentioned other camps last night."

"Yeah, what about them?"

"Do you have contact with them at all?"

"Yeah, we use old satellite radios. Why you asking?"

“Kimmy's family, they lived in Castleford, and I was wondering if we could find out if they are at another camp.”

He gives me a slightly pitying look as if he is about to give me some bad news. My heart sinks, I don't like that look one bit, what is he about to tell me? It couldn't be about Kimmy's family. He can't know who they are.

“We can try mate, but don't get your hopes up. Castleford was hit pretty hard after the bombs went off, there weren't many survivors if you see where I’m going.”

I can't believe it. He is telling me to prepare for the worst. Kimmy's family is most likely dead. The image of Kimmy's face absolutely heart-broken flashes into my mind.

“Please could you just run it by a few camps? Her dad’s name is Tommy. And last name Fisher. If anyone knows where they are…” Alex interrupts me, gasping out, “Old man Fisher! That hard bastard? Yeah he’s down in Wakefield.” He squints over at Kimmy. “He’s her old man?”

Joy rushes through my body. The way Alex describes him as a hard bastard tells me that is definitely the right man.

“So you have seen him? And his wife and son?”

“I can't say for them but I was on a hunt with Fisher about three weeks back when Wakefield needed a few extra hands. The man saved Mes' and my arses out there.”

I can't believe our luck. Now we knew for certain Tommy was alive. The news that her family are actually alive will just make this day perfect for her. If, I’m over-joyed, I can't imagine how Kimmy is going to feel. I can't wait to tell her and see that look of surprise and happiness on her face.

"We need to get in touch with him. Can we do that now?"

"I'll give John a shout, but he's busy making sure this place is secure for tonight and nobody gets on that radio without his word. Come on might be better if you are there to ask as well."

Alex sets off up the building but before I follow, Kimmy is smiling at me, still surrounded by the children. I smile back and gesture to let her know that I'm going off with Alex for a second. She nods and focuses back on the children. I catch up with Alex. To my shock, the front shutter is wide open and dozens of people are outside relaxing on the curb, in the sunlight, chatting, smoking and just hanging out.

My eyes adjust to the sunlight and I stand at the door for a second wondering if it is actually safe enough to go out. In the woods, I felt reasonably safe throughout the day because we were surrounded by trees and were in the middle of nowhere. But here in town, surrounded by empty and dark buildings, any of these buildings could have a lurker inside, analysing us and waiting for the sun to go down.

"You coming or what?" Alex shouts back to me as he heads down the street. I force myself out through the opening and take in the full situation. I can see men on the top of the buildings with rifles scoping out the place, keeping a watchful eye out over the innocent families and friends. They are pin-pointed at each corner of each building like it really is an army base, secured from every direction. Seeing all these men suddenly gives me a sense of safety, I never would have thought there would be this many people willing to fight and protect the people of this camp.

I catch up with Alex down the street.

"Here lad, you take this. Ya never know when it could come in handy."

he places a big silver handgun that was as heavy as two house bricks in my hand. It has a heavy black handle which says Desert Eagle 2.0. I say this aloud as I read it.

"Yep, a bullet from that thing will pierce through a lurker like a knife through butter mate. Try not to shoot ya self in your own leg though, ya wouldn't be much help hopping after lurkers with us, would ya?" he says, laughing. I'm not sure if I should be offended. It's as if he expects me to shoot myself in my leg by tucking it into my belt. I can't blame him for joking about with me like that though. I was training to be a lawyer so I don't exactly scream soldier.

"If ya don't already know, to kill 'em you need one shot to the heart and another to the brain. If ya don't destroy both, the damn things will heal in seconds and that just makes them angrier."

Around the corner, we find John with Mes and another group of soldiers.

John is issuing instructions. "I want hidden booby traps on each corner, of every street in a three block ratio. If they are blocks away, it will confuse them and give us the advantage of knowing where they are."

He signals to a man who shouts, "Right soldiers, you heard him. Off to it," which sends them all scattering. He turns to Mes, "Right Mes, what I want you to do is find volunteers to be pin pointed on the highest roofs with rifles."

He notices Alex and I as we approach and he turns towards us.

"Alex, Stuart." He nods as he acknowledges each of us. "You made up your mind yet, boy?"

That word again, boy. He keeps calling me that and it makes me feel like a small child, makes me feel helpless every time he calls me it. But I swallow my pride and don't say anything because he's not a man I could speak up to, especially not now when he's got a mission, which includes protecting me as well.

"I think Kimmy and I will stick around for now, sir."

"Our new friend has a request, John."

"He does, does he? I'm listening."

But before I can get a word out, Alex jumps in again.

"Guess who his girlfriend's dad has turned out to be?"

John inclines his head to Alex indicating he should carry on. "It's only big Tommy Fisher!"

Even John looks surprised for a second. "Tommy Fisher, aye? Good man, good soldier. And, if I remember right, you wouldn't be stood here now without him, would you, Alex"?

"Me neither," says Mes. "I owe that man me life."

I chip in, trying to be as polite as possible. "I was hoping to get in touch on one of your radios seeing as he doesn't know Kimmy and I survived and she really needs to know the rest of her family is ok?"

He looks at me as he considers my request.

"Because I owe that man for the life of these two soldiers, I will allow you to use it, but remember this is a one off. That radio is not for family chats so don't get used to it. Mes, you take them to it and get in touch with Wakefield Camp and let them know Fisher's daughter is here. Then you can go find your volunteers for sniping duty."

We head way back in, leaving Alex with John. I am excited to tell Kimmy about her dad and can't wait for her to be able to speak to him. Just as everything seems to be getting better, a man's voice shouts, "WEV'E GOT COMPANY, IN NOW."

It is one of the men on the roof and he is screaming to John and Alex who are sprinting back, ushering everybody into the back.

"Get in now!" Alex screams. Now there is a loud bang then another. The men on the roof are letting off shots. What could they be shooting at? It's the middle of the day so it can't be lurkers. Almost all the family is in through the door now, running. I hear Kimmy's voice screaming for me from inside. Alex grabs my shoulder, "Get in now, lad."

"What's going on?" But before I can get an answer, I see behind him and John and see a group of men running down the street faster than any human could possibly run. How does that make sense? These can't be lurkers. How could lurkers be running through the day?

"It's too late," Mes shouts. She rams the shutter down from outside, locking me, John, Alex and herself outside.

They all ready their guns and let off shot after shot but the lurkers just run through the bullets. I can hear Kimmy braying from the other side of the shutter. If they get past us, which does not seem unlikely right now, they will be inside in seconds. I can't just stand here doing nothing so I pull out the Desert Eagle Alex gave me and follow the others, shooting and shooting, hoping. A couple of lurkers drop from bullets from the snipers, but they are not going down fast enough. There are too many of them and only a few of us. They scream like rabid animals as they get closer. Nothing is going to stop these monsters. What's that? I hear gunfire from behind us, as all the men that scattered to set the traps come flying around the corner. Lurkers drop like flies, but it still is not enough.

Alex screams, "COME ON YOU FUCKING BEASTS." He pulls out a huge blade from goodness knows where and runs towards them. Mes follows after she throws a blade which suddenly is sticking through a lurker's head and he drops to the ground. But I cannot concentrate on them as a lurker comes flying towards me. I don't hesitate and swing the gun around like a club and bash him in the face. He stumbles to the ground. My body begins to boil and my eyes begin to feel like they are popping out of my head. I feel as if I can demolish a horse. A surge of power is rushing through me just like when the other lurker attacked Kimmy and I. I throw myself on top of this one and swing the gun blow after blow into his face until the screaming stops. My eyesight gone red as if blood is covering my eyes. I focus on stopping these things getting through that shutter to Kimmy. My lurker is dead so I look up and see men fighting lurkers but they are losing. One man is on the floor and a lurker tears out lumps from his neck. I grab a blade from the floor at the side of a dead soldier and swing at the lurker taking his head clean off. I hear Mes swearing and choking from where she is up against the wall, a lurker strangling her. Alex is trying to get to her and he chops through yet more lurkers like he is an unstoppable machine, but he is not going to make it. I take a few long strides and leap into the lurker holding Mes up and tackle him to the floor. He swings his hand around and suddenly I'm thrown over him. I'm skidding off down the path, but I can't let this beast win so I climb straight back up. Before I know it, he's grabbed my neck, lifted me from the ground and slammed me back down onto the pavement. But he's leaning over me so I reach up and stick the blade through his ribs. I throw him to the ground as I stagger back to my feet. Give him one big kick to the face, pull the knife from his ribs and stick it through his forehead, destroying the brain as well just like Alex told me too.

Everything goes quiet. All I hear is Alex scream for Mes and I turn around.

The anger I feel is unbearable. It is as if I could tear somebody apart. My head is in splitting pain again. I need to calm down, catch my breath. What the hell is happening to me? Why am I feeling like this? How could I do what I have just done? Breathe, Stuart, breathe. I repeat this over and over like a mantra. It's not going away. The pain moves down to my stomach. I scream out in pain and drop to the floor. This is agony. I can feel my body shaking. Hunger rips through me as if I have not eaten for a whole week, as if my stomach is turning in on itself, its acids turning on my stomach lining as it begins to eat itself. I can't breathe. And my body is still boiling. I cannot handle the pain. I need to eat something, I'm starving. Now, I feel like I'm choking. I can't breathe at all now. My vision blurs again. Intoxicating smells run up my nostrils and the pain grows drastically.

All of a sudden, I feel hands grab my face. "Stuart!" Kimmy screams. Of course, it's Kimmy. "Stuart, what's wrong?" She sounds frantic.

I try to push her away. "Kimmy, no. Stay away from me." My voice comes out in gasps as I fight through the pain.

She pins me to the floor, grabbing my cheeks with her hands.

"Stuart look at me. Breathe, Stuart, breathe."

It's the same phrase I was telling myself and it's proving as ineffectual. 'I'm trying. I'm trying for her. But the pain is over taking me. I need to get her away from me. I'm terrified that I am going to hurt her. "Please Kimmy, go. I can't."

She holds me even tighter and her face is millimetres from mine.

"Look at me. You're ok, Stuart. You are ok. I'm here. Breathe, Stuart." she says it again and again, as calmly as she is able and, miraculously, it starts to work. The pain diminishes slightly. She is calming me down. I open my eyes properly and the red vanishes. My vision clears gradually and then I can see her blue eyes staring into mine. Eventually a small breath makes its way through my airways. Then a bigger one follows. With the oxygen, my body begins to calm. I just stare into her eyes and everything begins to feel better. The pain is subsiding. She pulls me up, although I can't remember how I got to the ground, and she hugs me, placing her forehead gently against mine.

"You're ok, you're ok."

I can hear her sobs as she says it. There is a real pain in her voice. She must have thought that I was dying on the other side of that shutter. But how can I explain what I'm suspecting, that what just happened, that was not human. And to make matters worse, everything that happened to me, everybody must have seen. I close my eyes and hug Kimmy as tight as I can. She was the reason I came back from whatever just happened. She has brought me back from what I felt was going to be the end of my humanity.

"What's going on? Is he alright?" I hear Mes say.

Kimmy stares into my face as she holds my cheeks firmly in her hands. She spends a good few seconds thinking and then turns to the others.

"Yeah he's fine now. He's got asthma and that was a bad attack. He couldn't breathe at all but he's better now."

Kimmy and I both know this is a lie. Surely knowbody could believe this, I don't have asthma. I was perfectly healthy before the bite and I can tell that Kimmy knows what happened to me wasn't human, but she loves me too much to risk telling them the truth.

Mes comes over as Kimmy and I separate and grabs my arm pulling me up.

"You are one crazy bastard, Stuart. I give ya that. Not a lot of civilians would jump into a fist fight with a lurker." She shakes her head slightly, still in disbelief. I realise then they must have believed Kimmy's story, "You saved my arse." She shakes my hand firmly in thanks and then Alex shakes my hand as well.

"Ya saved my sister mate. I don't know how to begin to repay ya."

John shouts out, saving me from having to reply to their thanks, "Right soldiers, enough celebrating, we've lost people. This isn't a victory in my eyes."

As one, everybody lowers their head in respect and shame. I look over Alex's shoulder and there are five corpses half torn apart by the lurkers. Some lurkers are dead as well. The others seem to have fled.

I still can't get my head around how they were running in direct sunlight.

"What the hell was that?" I ask. Does anyone wanna explain how lurkers were running in the day?"

It goes even quieter. Alex turns back to me. "They weren't full lurkers, Stuart, they were in transition."

"Transition?" My stomach drops as things begin to make sense.

"If a person is bitten, they either die, or they become a lurker. But it happens over days. They transition, some humans, pethetic humans, work for the lurkers in hopes of been changed"

The shock hits me like a tidal wave. Everything is finally fully clear to me. Kimmy squeezes my hand. We both have just found out exactly what is happening to me, the rage the strength, the healing. It all suddenly makes sense. I'm becoming what I have been fighting to survive against. I'm becoming a blood feeding monster and soon, I will not be able to help it, like the ones that just attacked us. They were rabid animals fuelled by the same feelings consuming me before Kimmy calmed me down. It could be a matter of hours before I change fully and attack someone. I inwardly gasp, what if that someone is Kimmy? I could never live with myself if I did. I can't risk this. It's clear to me I need to get out of here as soon as the base is quiet again. I need to get away from everyone, away from Kimmy.

Chapter 7

John has told everyone to go in their rooms while some volunteers clean up the street and collect the bodies. Kimmy and I rush to our room as fast as we can. As soon as I shut the door fully, Kimmy breaks down on the bed, tears streaming down both cheeks uncontrollably, trying the catch her breath between sobs. I know I need to comfort her but how can I? What could I possibly say to make the situation we are in any better? I'm gradually becoming a monster. She knows it. I know it. It's just a matter of time. And we both know that when I change fully, I will no longer be me. The man she fell in love with will be gone forever. I might as well be dying right here in front of her. There is nothing that can be done to stop me from going away.

I slowly walked over and sat beside Kimmy. I lift her gently, pull her head onto my chest and wrap myself around her. I can't say anything. Speechless, I just look up to the roof, holding back my own tears, stroking her hair. Hate for the situation we are in rises up through me. How could things become this bad?

How has the world become a battlefield filled with monsters? And now I am on my way to becoming one of these monsters.

“Kimmy,” I whisper into her ear.

She calms down a little bit and the sobbing stops. She lets a little murmur of acknowledgement.

“I have to leave.” I don't know why I tell her. I should just slip away when she's asleep which would make things easier for the both of us. But the habit of years of being candid and open with her are clearly hard to break. I guess I want to give her a proper goodbye before I disappear to die alone. I want my last memory with Kimmy to be a nice one. After this moment, I will never see her again. The simple thought of never seeing her again brings tears to my eyes and I have to stop my lip from quivering. A hole opens up in my heart as I think about it.

She raises her head and stares at me with her wide eyes, clearly showing the hurt within them and now also burning red from all her tears.

“What? No. Why? No, you have to stay here we can do something. There must be something we can do. I’m not giving up this easily.”

She continues to rant. I can't handle seeing her like this, it hurts so much, but I need to get this out of the way.

“Babe, stop, please, I can't stay here. I’m going to become one of them and when I do, I will no longer be able to control myself. I can’t risk anything happening to you.”

“No! You can't leave me Stuart, please. I need you. My life is with you.”

“It can't be. Not anymore. I have to go, Kimmy. It’s not safe for anyone as long as I am here."

"I'll come with you then. We'll leave together, fight this together."

I need to help her process things quicker, help her come to terms with it somehow, but how can I? The reality just dropped on us like a bomb and I can't process all the implications. I have to make the right decision fast as much as it pains me to see her pleading. I place my hand on her right cheek and wipe away the tears, gently kiss her.

"No, Kimmy. You can't come with me; your life is here now. You will be safe here."

"There is nothing for me here if you are not here," she snaps back, her tears drier, her voice stronger.

I remembered that she did not know her dad was alive and just a few towns away. That made me feel better, knowing that she will not be alone among strangers without me here. And it will give her something else to think about, someone else to hang on to through these tough times. That's some good news for her to help her feel better right now.

"Yes, there is, Kimmy. I didn't have time to tell you before. I know your family are alive. They are at a camp in Wakefield."

"What?" she replies, thrown, and then accusative. "How do you know that?"

"I asked Alex, this morning, as I promised. Turns out he knows ya dad and John said you can speak to him on the radio when it calms down after the attack."

She goes quiet, too quiet. I was expecting more happiness than this but she is muted, wide-eyed. She just sits there, staring at the ground.

"That's great," she eventually says, nearly whispering the words.

"Babe, your family's alive. That is great. You won't be alone."

She looks up at me with the straightest look on her face. I have never seen her face this serious. Tears begin to leak from her eyes again.

"I will be alone if you're not here. You're my family too, Stuart. I can't lose you."

My eyes begin to fill up too. I can't help it. The look she is giving me is unbearable. I can't take it in. My lips quiver as I say "I'm sorry." My whole body chokes up as I say it. I can't hold back the tears anymore.

I have to stand up and turn away from her. I can't let her see me lose focus my determination. I can't show weakness if I want her to be strong, if I want her to let me go.

"If there was anything I could do to stay with you, I would do it, Kimmy. I love you so much. You are my everything, so I've got to do this. To keep you safe."

She stands up too and firmly grabs me by my arms. "Stuart, this isn't up for discussion. I'm not gonna let you go off by yourself. You think that when you fully transition, you'll be this unstoppable monster but you won't. You'll still be the same kind and gentle man who I fell in love with. You'll have a choice to become a monster or not, like the lurker in the petrol station. He let us go. He chose to help us."

I had forgotten about him. My memory flashes back to how he allowed us to walk away from him. Unlike the other lurkers, he did not attack first. He questioned me, threatened me but he did not attack. He had no intention of eating us or attacking us. He would have shot us rather than bitten us. Kimmy was right about one thing, he must have had a choice. There was a human inside who could control his anger and primal urges, and if he could, maybe I could too? But I still can't stay here to find out. It would be too risky. I will leave but at least now I have some hope that I might try and control myself away from danger.

I place my hands behind Kimmy's head and rest our foreheads together. I gaze intensely into her big blue eyes. I rub the tears away from her cheeks with my thumbs. I gently whisper, "You are right, Kimmy. Maybe I could try and fight this, and I will, but I have to do it alone. I can't risk hurting you or anybody else. Knowing that you are here and safe will make it easier for me to concentrate on fighting it. Please stay here or be with your family and maybe, one day, I will be able to come back. But you have got to let me go for now, Kimmy, please, I need you to do this for me. Don't make it harder than it already is."

"What if ya don't ever come back? You think I'm going to be ok here with my family, but every day I'm going to be thinking, wondering if you're ok, not knowing where you are or if you're even alive! Ya can't ask me to live like that Stuart. Ya just can't, it will be too painful. There's got to be another way."

She's not going to let this go. I can tell she will never be ok with me leaving and how could I expect her to be? For the last ten months, all we have had is each other, nothing else has seemed to matter as long as we were together. And now I'm going to vanish, leave her somewhere new and unfamiliar and I have no idea where I'm going to go or even any plan for how I am going to begin to beat this thing.

The door knocks then suddenly swings open. Mes is on the other side. She can see we have been crying, it would be hard to hide even if the tears weren't still streaking our faces. Kimmy's eyes are bright red and puffy and mine are probably the same.

“You two ok?” she asks, sounding concerned.

All of a sudden, I can smell something. It is a mouth-watering smell and as it gets stronger, it becomes the most beautiful thing I’ve ever smelled. I don’t know where its coming from. Kimmy says something to Mes at the edge of my hearing but I don’t pay attention, just a mumble, my mind is concentrating on this smell too much, this unbelievable smell. Where is it coming from? My stomach rumbles, I have to find out what it is. I walk out of the door, past Mes and the smell gets even stronger and a sudden hit of flavours run through my mind but there's no one around with any food anywhere. Alex is stood close by, directing the men through carrying the bodies, but there is nobody else in sight. I close my eyes and concentrate on sniffing, trying to pinpoint the direction but it’s all over the place, it’s excruciating. It’s like the halls are filled with freshly baked cakes and I can't see them. It’s torture, driving me insane. I feel my shoulder being pulled back which brings me back to reality. I swing around and open my eyes to see Mes staring at me. My eyes burn but then I come too and the smell goes and the burn disappears.

“Stuart?” Mes says, with fear in her voice. She takes a long look at me, backing away from me slowly.

“What’s wrong?” I ask. The look on her face scares me. It’s like she’s looking at a ghost.

Kimmy walks towards me shivering and hesitant to come closer. “Stuart, how do you feel?” She looks serious. What is wrong with everybody? I feel fine.

“I feel fine Kimmy, why?” It’s probably best if I don’t tell Mes I was ignoring her trying to track down that heavenly food. She might think it rude.

“It’s happening, Stuart,” she replies to me, pointedly and then anxiously looks around at everybody else. I hesitate to reply but then the truth hits me. My change is happening now. That smell, that hypnotizing smell must have brought it on while I was concentrating on it. But I feel fine. I don't have any pain or boiling rage of anger like the other times. This time it's different, I just feel normal. There's a mirror on the wall just past our room. I slowly walk up and look into it, and the shock hits me like a slap to the face. My eyes, my eyes are shining like those of the lurkers I have seen before. It's as if I have two lights behind each eye. All of a sudden, my situation becomes so real I can feel my self beginning to panic. The hallway feels like it is getting smaller. I feel claustrophobic. I need to get out of here now. This can't happen, not here not now, not with everybody around to see me become the thing we hate so much. I look back to Kimmy in fear and desperation.

Mes screams to Alex, "He's one of them, Alex!"

Kimmy shouts to me, "Go!" But every inch of my body is stuck, my feet are nailed to the floor. I can't believe this has happened already. I wanted to be far away by the time it did. But now, there is only one way out, through Alex and the men. I can't do this, I can't fight them. Alex pulls out his hand gun and points it straight at my forehead.

Kimmy screams at him, "No, Alex, don't! Stuart what ya doing? Run, please."

I can hear the plea but I can't do this. I don't want to live as a monster. I can't live without Kimmy. Life will never be the same again. My life is already over, I might as well let Alex make it permanent. There's no getting out of here now, the door is blocked by soldiers with cocked guns. I give up, my body relaxes, the panic stops. I just look towards Kimmy. I want her to be the last thing I ever see.

"I love you," I say gently. She drops to her knees, crying. "I love you too, Stuart," she says back. I close my eyes; I don't want to see it coming. I nod, giving Alex permission to end me. I hear a bang and then my body goes numb. I hear Kimmy sobbing hysterically, crying out my name, but the sound fades until I can no longer hear her voice.

I can't explain this feeling. I know I have been shot but I still feel awake. There is nothing but darkness but I am still conscious, I can still think, still ask the question, "what is happening to me?" I feel at peace, calm and comfortable. Is this the passing over stage you hear about? Am I going to suddenly wake up in a different place in the afterlife? Could there actually be a heaven and hell and I am going to wake up in either one of them? It is easier to believe now, given everything that has happened. These lurkers could be hellish demons after all, with no real life but creating more evil than anything in this world.

***

I hear a voice. It's growing stronger, but I still can't make out what it is saying. All I hear is a mumble, but then it becomes clear. My name. I hear "Stuart" repeated, getting louder, then a light shines into my eyes bringing me back to consciousness. It shines so bright that I can only see the light, my vision is entirely the light. Then a sudden rush of pain in my chest shocks me into full presence. It's awful, like something is digging around in my body. Suddenly my mouth opens and I scream from the chest pain. My eyes adjust to the light. Everything is still blurry but I can clearly tell that its Mes above me. Hands are cupping my face pulling my head back whilst Alex is digging in my chest. The pain is horrific, I let out another scream before composing myself enough to ask, "What are you doing?"

"Shut up." The words come from Alex. "Stop moving around. It's gonna be more painful the more you move."

But I can't help it, I feel trapped and my body convulses from the pain trying to break free. Then I realize, I am bound to a chair, straps attaching my arms to the rests and my legs tied to the legs.

"What's going on Alex? Where am I?" It meant to come out as calm as I could manage but I ended up screaming at him. Then I feel the thing in my chest suddenly pulled out with force, I gasp and then take a deep breath. As I do, Mes releases my head and I can see Alex stood holding a metal device like tongs with a crushed bullet in the end. I catch my breath and the pain fades away so fast it's as if there was nothing ever there. I look at my chest and whatever wound had been open there before has disappeared and fully healed. My skin is smooth and unblemished.

"You're lucky, Stuart," Alex says but I have no idea what he could mean because nothing about the situation seems lucky to me.

"Why?" I reply.

"You are lucky you have a girl that loves you so much. I was gonna put a bullet straight through your head, put you out your misery, but your lass wouldn't give up. She snatched up Mes' gun and put it to my head, so we decided to give her what she wants, give you a chance."

"A chance? A chance for what?"

I don't understand. It is clear I am now a lurker, the instant healing is the last piece of proof. There is no cure so what possible chance could they be looking for? I am no longer human. I am the enemy as far as they are concerned.

"To show us that you're still one of us. I would never go for it. As far as I'm concerned, you're one of them now, and when you get the chance, I believe you will try kill us all. I don't think you'll be able to fight what you are now. And you are a killer now Stuart no matter what you might think, but Kimmy made a good argument on your behalf. You didn't attack us and you did save my sister’s life, so we’ll see. We’ll give you a chance.”

“Where's Kimmy?” “You are not seeing her just yet, and believe me mate, ya don't want her to see what you’re gonna be going through.”

“Why? What are you going to do with me?” I have visions of painful experiments to get the lurker out of me.

“We’re not gonna do anything. You are gonna do it to yourself. See all we are gonna do is keep ya locked in here. You are gonna starve. And then, when your lust for blood is at its highest, you’ll have to fight against it, and if by any miracle you can, then I might think about letting you live.”

But just like before, I don't feel any different. I still feel human, I have no urge to attack Mes or Alex. I feel no lust to tear them apart as I have seen other lurkers do in the past. The simple image of feeding on them forces itself into my mind but it makes me feel sick. I could not imagine myself wanting to do that.

“I don't have any lust for blood, I still feel fine. I swear.”

“Really? Let’s see, shall we?”

He bangs on the door and a man I don’t recognise comes in wheeling a small metal trolley. He leaves it in front of me, then walks out. As I breathe in through my nose, the smell I had been chasing earlier comes back and gets stronger. can feel my eyes begin to burn as it gets closer. Then the man walks in with a bowl and my mouth waters and my eyes begin to glaze over. They are glued with concentration on this bowl. He places it in front of me and now I can see that the bowl is full of blood, and the smell is stronger than ever and all I want to do is pick up this bowl and drink. I want it to glug down my throat and fill my mouth with the taste and fill my stomach with it. Just thinking about it makes me feel stronger and pleasured. My mouth widens trying to suck the taste through the air. It mesmerises me. But then I feel something which snaps me out of it, just a little pressure on my bottom lip. With my tongue, I feel two pointed fangs and they are hanging out of my mouth. I can't process this, the smell from this bowl is too strong. I can feel my body begin to shake, my lips quivering, my eyes burning harder than ever. I cannot bring myself to look away from this bowl; I have never seen or smelled anything as beautiful in my life.

"Look at yourself," I hear Alex say in disgust. Then a loud bang brings my attention away from the bowl. They have slammed the door and left me alone with this bowl of blood directly in front of me. I scan the room, trying desperately not to stare at the blood but there's nothing else but four close walls and a thick steel door with a small window at the top, and me in the middle, tied to a steel chair.

I feel sweat begin to pour from my forehead and even though I am not looking at the bowl, the image is in my mind. I can't help but picture myself lowering my head within the rim and licking it all up like a cat, ingesting every single drop. My eyes go back to the bowl and the pain grows in my stomach again. It's horrible. The need to drink it overwhelms me. My arms try to break free. Nothing matters to me but getting to this bowl, getting this blood into my body. My head burns, my eyes feel like they are going to pop out of my head.

Suddenly I find myself running round chasing somebody. I grab them and spin them around and it's Mes but with no hesitation, I tear straight into her and rip her throat out and let the blood flow out from her into my mouth and down my throat. I feel the warmth slide down my throat into my stomach and I have never felt so much pleasure in my life and I can't stop myself from grabbing her throat again, my fangs sinking into her skin deliciously and I suck the blood out of her until there is nothing left to take. I have never felt so happy. I have the biggest, bloodiest smile on my face, relishing in the joy of all of it.

A slap across my face brings me out of my dream. Alex is back again, then I come to terms with the fact that I am still in the room, shackled to the chair. I have not moved, which means that everything I was just feeling was a dream, a beautiful dream that desperately I want to come true.

"How are you feeling, Stuart? You wanna tear me apart yet?"

"How long have I been here?"

It couldn't have been that long, it felt like I was just staring at the bowl a few minutes ago before I pictured myself feeding of Mes. But my body feels weak and worn out and I can barely lift my head.

"Two days," he says.

I look up at Alex in shock but my gaze zeroes in on his neck, or more specifically the jugular vein popping out of his neck. I can actually see the blood flowing through it like a drink through a straw. I want to slash it open and drain the straw dry, drain Alex dry. My arm swings loose from the chair. I break free and grab Alex by the throat and pushing him up against the wall, and my fangs bite into his neck, breaking open the vein and I drink up every drop of blood from his body, but then I feel another slap on my face and realise it was yet another dream and not real.

"You are not sleeping through this. Open your fucking eyes!"

He shouts at me grabbing me by the chin and giving me another huge slap across the face, fully waking me up. A rush of anger consumes me and I lunge for him with my fangs.

"I'll fucking kill you! Let me go now!" I scream at him. The anger in me forces me to shout these things out. I know what I am saying is not me but I do not care, if I was loose, I would kill him and I would feed on him. There would be no stopping me and I would love it.

"You wanna kill me Stuart?" he asks.

I begin to laugh. "I would gladly tear your head clean off and drain you dry. You are nothing, you hear me nothing! Now let me fucking go."

He smirks at me with this infuriating grin which makes me want to attack him even more and makes me frustrated to my very last nerve. He opens the door and walks out talking to someone outside. "You sure ya wanna go in?"

"Yeah I need to see him."

"That's not Stuart in there, Kimmy," I hear him warn her but she does not listen and walks in slowly. I'm looking at the floor so I can only see her shoes. I force myself not to look up.

"Stuart," she says gently but I can sense the small tremble of fear.

"Get the fuck out of here Kimmy."

"No, look at me, Stuart. It's me, look at me."

I look up but I don't look in her eyes, my eyes automatically go to her neck just as they did with Alex.

"Stuart, I know this is not you. You can beat this. Look at me, I'm begging you try to fight it, please!"

I can hear her words but all I can smell is fresh blood and I can hear her heart beating, pushing her life force through, and all I want to do is drain her of life.

“I don’t want to fight it, you stupid cow. I can hear everything,” I linger on the words. I don’t sound like me. “I can smell all the blood in your body. I can smell everything that is going on in your body. It’s amazing.” I pause. “And all I want to do is tear you limb from limb.”

She starts to tear up, trying to hold the tears back.

“You don't mean that Stuart.” She tries to sound convinced herself.

Again, I begin to laugh. I am not able to stop these things from coming out of my mouth. It’s like there’s another person inside me and they are the one controlling which words leave my mouth.

She stiffens and grows more firm with me.

“I don’t care what you say, Stuart. I know that’s not you. The real you loves me and would not hurt anybody, and I'm going to bring him back, I don’t care if I’ve got to lock you in here for a whole year.”

I can’t sit here for a whole year dreaming about blood. This torture needs to stop. I can’t live like this. How could I say such things to Kimmy? She's right, I do love her and I would never have hurt her before but that’s not me anymore. I am no longer the man I was. I'm a monster now and I don't think I'm going to be able to beat this. The lust is too strong.

“Kimmy, Kimmy I cant resist this. You need to kill me, or let the others kill me. The pain is too much. Please it hurts, Kimmy it hurts so much.”

“No. You need to fight this.”

She starts to leave and the fact that she is ignoring me makes my blood boil. I don't want this anymore; I didn’t choose this in the first place. Another two days of this will drive me insane and the pain is already unbearable.

“Kimmy, you fucking bitch, don't leave! Kill me now, Kimmy. Ya can't do this to me. Kill me now. I will fucking kill you, you bitch!”

But she doesn’t turn around, she just keeps walking out of the door and slams it shut on me.

The room is silent now as soon as the reverberations cease. The smell still lingers filling the whole room. I can't handle this, it feels like my stomach is consuming itself and my head is getting crushed by two sledge hammers as it pounds. I need to fight it, nothing is going to stop this pain but me. Kimmy is not going to let the others put me out of my misery. I try picturing Kimmy stroking my head like she would as she tried to calm me down, focusing on her own breathing, taking long slow breaths so that mine might match up. I can’t control what I imagine. I can’t grasp this image of Kimmy. The smell of the blood in front of me is overpowering and images flash unbidden through my head, all of me killing again. But I fight it screaming inside my head: “STOP, STOP!” I try to breath slowly but I can’t it’s like a continuous panic attack. Sweat pours from my head uncontrollably. I can't take this anymore. With the last bit of sanity I have left, I let out another huge scream using my whole body this time, tensing every single muscle in my body so hard that it hurts. I can feel the rage leaving my body as I scream and I keep screaming until my lungs have nothing left in them. I continue to try to scream but choke on my own breathless lungs. I manage to take one deep breath and slowly let it out. As I continue with every breath, I can feel my body becoming more and more relaxed luring me into a deeper and deeper state of self-control overcoming the anger rushing through my body.

Chapter 8

I have no idea how long it has been since Kimmy was in the room. My whole body is aching just trying to keep my mind straight. I have concentrated on my breathing for what feels like forever, but the smell of the bowl is still there, trying to pull the monster from inside of me. I have a new self-control and I am determined to defeat these cravings. The way I spoke to Kimmy when she was in here with me was horrible. That did not feel like me and I can't allow that person to come out again.

There have been times during this torture when everything feels calm and peaceful and I can hear quiet talking from the other side of the door. I couldn't understand what they were saying for the most part but every now and again I would hear certain words as if they were in the room talking right in front of me, just like when Kimmy and I first came into town and I could hear voices talking right around the corner. Maybe it's an effect of the infection, another dark gift that lurkers possess to make them better predators in the night, to make them better hunters.

I could actively try to use this gift which at least would give something to concentrate on and try hear what is going on out there. I could see how Kimmy is doing without her having to see me like this. Every time my hearing has enhanced before has happened when I close my eyes, breathe slowly and concentrate on that breathing, blocking everything else out. I try this now. I close my eyes and breathe. There's not the slightest noise except for the gentle movement of my chest rising and falling. Despite the base teeming with people. I concentrate harder and feel a slight twitch in my ears. Now I can hear noises but it is just noise. I can't make sense of any of it. It sounds like a man talking, but wait, now it is getting stronger, a little clearer. It's a low strong voice and I recognise it. Yes, it is John. There's no doubt in my mind now; I know that is John, it's so clear now.

"…suns down now Alex, we've got to be careful. That attack the other morning might not be the one we were expecting, it could still happen tonight."

"What do ya want me to do?" Alex replies.

"The men are in position, the building is secured, traps are up on each block surrounding the camp. There's not much more we can do now but be hyper vigilant for what could come."

Another attack could happen, I never even thought about that while I was trapped inside. The lurker on the camera, he was not there the other morning. I would have noticed his eyes, those eyes which felt so familiar.

"How is she doing, sis" I hear Alex say.

Are they talking about Kimmy? I listen intently.

"Not good at all, she won't talk to anybody."

John replies with his characteristic lack of sympathy. "She needs to be straight-headed now. If we have an attack tonight, she needs to be ready to move, sharpish."

"Ya can't blame her for being how she is, sir. The man she loves is a few rooms down from here, growling like a beast trying to eat her. She's going to take some time to process that and amongst strangers too."

Alex speaks up, "Stuart mentioned her dad, big Tommy Fisher at Wakefield camp, could ya radio through? Give the poor lass something to look forward to for tomorrow? Anything to take her mind off Stuart…"

At least they are looking after her. I thought they might have judged her harshly for keeping my infection a secret and allowing me to nearly fully change within their walls.

"Mes, make it happen."

I listen more intently. John and Alex's voices get lower and fade out along with their footsteps but I pick up other sounds, a woman singing to her child, people talking, but it's all getting too much. There are too many voices, it's scrambled in my head, just a big noise, sensory overload. All of them filter through my ears and I can't stop it, all these sounds getting louder and louder and I can't differentiate between them. They drill into my head and spin around inside my brain, painfully. I try to fight it but it is not stopping, just getting louder and more painful. I can hear far too many people at once. I'm not used to this. My ears weren't designed for this. It hurts. But then suddenly, when I really cannot take it anymore and just want to curl up, my arms straining at their bonds to cover my ears, it stops. I can only hear hushed crying. It isn't a painful cry, just one that screams desperation. I know her too well not to recognise it. It sounds like Kimmy is ready to give up.

"Please god," she says in between sobs.

"Please don't take him away from me. This isn't fair, please bring him back," she begs.

My eyes fill up and there's no stopping the tears pouring from my eyes. I don't even want to try. The pain in her voice. I thought I was going through torture in here whilst she was out there, looked after and waiting for me to come to terms with what I am and fight it like I should have tried doing from the start. But she is in a worse hell than me. She has to stand around not being able to help in any way whilst I turn. I forgot how this would affect her. I was just concentrating on the blood, the smell of that fucking bowl of blood in front of me, distracting me from what really matters and why I should really be fighting these symptoms. It's not to stop the pain for myself but to stop the hurt and torture this is putting Kimmy through, to show her that the man she loves is still in here. I am not going to leave her.

I hear a bang at the door.

"Kimmy? It's Mes. Can I come in?"

She must be about to tell her that she can talk to her dad on the radio. She needs this, something to bring her a small amount of joy. I am not giving in now. I am going to fight this for Kimmy, even if I can't be with her because of what I am. I will not let her see me become a monster. Suddenly another smell brushes past my nose distracting me from listening to them, but it's not blood or any other smell I have encountered before, certainly not with this heightened sense of smell. It's horrid like a rotten sandwich or mouldy food. Again, I close my eyes to focus and the smell gets stronger and becomes so bad that it burns my nostrils. However, like everything else I get used to it, enough to pin point and concentrate. It's not coming from the building. It's such a horrible smell, like something decomposing, meat… then it dawns on me that it is the smell of a rotten dead body. And not just one, dozens of rotten bodies getting closer. It has to be the lurkers. The one on the camera must be coming back. I need to tell them, need to tell someone.

"Alex? John?" I shout as loudly as I can. "Alex! Alex quick, please. Alex!"

The door swings open.

"What the fuck do you want?" he shouts at me.

"Ya need to get everyone out of here now," I try to say calmly while panicking.

"What? Why?"

"They're coming. I can smell them, dozens of them, lurkers."

"Am gonna believe you, am I?"

"Please, get everyone out of here now, get fucking Kimmy out of here. They're coming. I'm not lying. Why would I lie?"

John comes running in.

"What's going on."

"John, you have to get everyone out of here now. Lurkers. Dozens of them. Ya have to believe me. They're coming."

He gives me a look as he thinks quickly. I can tell he still does not fully believe me. For all they know I could be leading them out into a quicker death, an ambush.

"Please John, I'm not lying. Get Kimmy out of here, now."

He signals to Alex who runs out the room spurring everyone into action. "Everybody up, now! We're moving, quick. Follow the escape plan to leave camp. This isn't a drill."

"I can't cut ya loose though, Stuart" John says to me with more sympathy in his face than I expect.

"Forget me. You just better not let anything happen to her, do you hear me?" He gives me a nod and runs to organise his people, slamming the door behind him.

The smell is still growing, getting closer. Now I can hear growls and grunts, the same noises I would make when imagining how the blood in the bowl would taste, but now the bowl means nothing to me. They need to hurry up and get everybody out of here. This is not like the last attack before I was locked away in here. There are more of them this time. I can hear every single one of them screaming and growling with one thing on their mind and that is food, and they will not stop at anything. Having felt the desire myself, I understand them better. Their lust will take over everything.

A huge bang outside my door. Kimmy is braying on the door, desperate to get through but before she can, I hear someone large grab her and pull her away. Is it John? It's sounds like his footfall. I will them to hurry. The lurkers are nearly here. Please, Kimmy stop fighting him, just run, please.

The lurkers ram into the shutters. I hear the whole building shudder and the crash against metal. Wave after wave of uncontrollable maniacs rip and tear at the metal sheets, they will be through in a matter of minutes. Kimmy is still here, I can hear her screams. I need to break free to make sure she gets out safely. I pull at the metal wire tying me to the chair, using every muscle in my body. My extra strength shakes the steel chair arms. I'm using so much strength, the metal begins to dig into my arms causing them to bleed, but it does not faze me, they will heal. I need to break free. I pull and pull tearing my arms more and more as the minutes fly by, It's too late. I hear the shutters give way and the monsters pile in one after another. There is screaming, gunshots. growls, bodies slamming to the floor. The image of Kimmy not getting out runs on a loop through my mind. I try one last huge pull and manage to tear the whole arm of the chair from the main frame. As I fling my arm in front of me, I knock the bowl of blood onto the floor where it spills but I have more urgent thoughts than the smell of the blood spreading over the floor. I swing my arm around and use it to release the other and tear myself free, quickly tearing the wire around my legs. I jump up to the door, adrenaline stopping my body from shaking after days trapped in that chair, and drag it open and see the damage.

There are soldiers on the floor, torn apart, all over the place in just the matter of seconds since the lurkers entered. I can see lurkers further down the building, feeding on a woman. I can see blonde hair and panic.

I run towards them, grabbing a blade from a dead soldier's hands. Two lurkers turn around but before they can even blink, I swing and take both their heads off in a single sweep, blood spraying all over my face. Shocked as I am at my new strength and abilities, I can't pause to reflect. I look down hoping this body is not Kimmy. I turn her around and it is the woman I saw with her baby, who smiled at me when we first came here. My relief to find it is not Kimmy is bittersweet. This is not fair. Innocent women and children all become meals for these rabid animals. I look around and families are dead on the floor. I tried to warn them but I wasn't fast enough to let them get out. I run round the building, checking the bodies but I can't see Kimmy anywhere, or John for that matter.

Where are all the lurkers? There were more than two at that shutter. I could smell and hear every single one of them. Now I can't.

It's all happened so fast. I don't know where they all could have gone. Then I hear the sound of vehicles screeching around the corner echoing into the building. I run outside and see a few trucks flying down the street about three blocks away. Kimmy and the rest of them must be in them. Suddenly the sound of another shutter door tears open from the inside. Four lurkers come flying out and chase down the street after the trucks. They can move much faster than the trucks. I have no doubt that they will catch them if they keep that speed up. I set off after them. If they can run that fast, I can too. The strength I have is becoming more natural to me and stride after stride I gain speed. Before I know it, I've passed one block and am halfway down the next. A quick glance to my side shows the windows as quick blurs flying past me. It feels effortless. The wind barely makes a sound as I glide through like I am flying. It's amazing how fast I can move, it seems like a dream.

Before I know it, the lurkers are in front of me and the trucks a little further ahead. We're gaining on them too quickly. I come up to the right of one of the lurkers and take the blade in my left hand and swing it into his neck, slicing his head clean off. He never even saw it coming, to him I was just another lurker chasing down the trucks with them. One of the lurkers saw me take out the other, processes this at lightning speed, and comes running into me so fast I can't even brace myself for the impact. We both go skidding across the floor and straight into a solid wall. He grabs me by my head trying to twist my neck around but I thrust the blade through his chest before he can, pushing him down onto his knees. I stand up as quickly as I can and thrust my hand into his neck tearing with my nails as much as I can out of his neck, unsure if that will kill him I grab the blade and with one huge swipe take off his head. I have to catch the other two.

I sprint down the street, turn the corner and run straight into the two lurkers who are waiting there for me.

One grabs me by my throat which stops instantly. He holds me in mid-air for a second and then throws me up against the lamp post. I hit it with an audible crack. It feels like my spine breaks and, as well as an overwhelming stabbing pain, I lose control of my arms and legs for a second. I nearly pass out from it but I need to keep myself awake. Before I can do anything, the other lurker throws his fist into my face. This succeeds in keeping me awake. It also crushes my whole face, my nose breaking and forced to the left side of my face, causing me to lose balance and fall to the floor. They pick me back up easily and throw me up against the building.

"A human-loving immortal? Pathetic," one of them spits.

My eyesight clears up and then just as I can see their faces, I hear the screech of a truck and then a bang, followed by a small explosion.

The idea that Kimmy might be on that truck spurs me on. I feel strength and anger boil up in me and red takes over once again. I grab the one that has me by the throat and throw him to the ground, and then pin the other one up against the lamp-post, sticking my fangs straight through his throat and tearing out lumps of flesh, This causes him to scream out in pain. I drop him to the ground. The other rises and charges at me but my hand automatically grabs his throat and I pick him up off the floor and slam his whole body onto the concrete with so much force that the concrete cracks around his body. I waste no time and slam my foot onto his head crushing his face and rendering him unconscious. I can't even recognise myself. The old me could never have even thrown a punch in a fight, let alone crush people without blinking. The ferocity that comes naturally is unbelievable. It all seems too natural to me somehow.

I hear the other one groaning behind me and, before he can heal himself sitting up against the post holding his neck, I jump behind him, my hand over his mouth and I pull his head back with all the force I can muster which tears his head clean off his neck. The rage in me gradually subsides as I realise what I've just done, able to see the inside of his neck in all its gory details. The brutality, the decapitation, hits me like a slap to the face bringing me back and making me gag. It blurs the red and the anger which had boiled up within me so quickly in the aftermath of the thought of Kimmy's death. But I haven't the time to dwell in horror. I need to find her.

I swing back towards the direction of the crash. I smell smoke and I set off running as fast as I can in that direction, skidding around the corners and in a matter of seconds I reach where the scene of the crash. Alex is sat on the floor with Mes laid across his legs. The truck crashed into a shop wall, crushing the whole front of the truck.

"Mes, wake up, please, wake up," Alex says frantically, holding her face and shaking her, trying to get a reaction. He notices me approach.

He raises his gun and points it at me. "Don't you come near her. Stay back."

I stay where I am, listening for her heartbeat. Alex is still screaming but I filter out his voice and concentrate on her and the sounds coming from her body. I hear a small weak beat so she is still alive.

"Get the fuck back, Stuart. I will shoot ya."

I put my hands up to show him that I mean no harm. There is blood everywhere from the bodies in the crash and, although I can smell it, it does not have an effect on me. All I need to do is make sure that Kimmy is safe but I can't see her here.

"Alex, I'm not gonna hurt anyone. Calm down. I'm on your side."

"Fucking calm down? My sister's dead, Stuart! They killed her." He drops the gun and hugs her close.

"She's not dead, Alex." He looks up at me, shocked. "What?"

"I can hear her heartbeat from here. She's alive, but barely. Is Kimmy on one of the other trucks?"

He ignores me and returns to trying to wake Mes up.

"Alex!" I shout and he jumps, I can see the minor reaction as if he moved a whole metre. I need to know if Kimmy is safe.

"Was Kimmy on one of the other trucks, is she safe?"

"Yeah, she was with John. They got away."

My whole body relaxed as relief swept over me. The rush, the fear, the anger all faded away and I dropped to my knees. I was assuming the worst and now knowing she's safe and probably on her way to see her dad and rest of the family gives me comfort. She will be safe with Tommy. He will die before he lets anything happen to her.

"Stuart, she's not coming around. What are we gonna do?"

It feels strange Alex asking me this, a little plea for help, no longer treating me like the enemy he has for the last few days. His voice is softer in his desperation. I need to help Alex now that I know Kimmy is safe. But he is lying out in the middle of the road at night with his half-dead sister in his lap. I have no idea how he is still alive or even how the lurkers who caused the crash left them here, alive, but there is no time to think about that now.

I approach cautiously but even still Alex reacts and jumps slightly as he notices. I can see he still does not trust me.

"Alex, ya need to let me help you. Trust me, I am ok. I will not hurt you or your sister. I give you my word."

He still hesitates but he lifts her with what energy he has and passes her to me. I take her from him and cradle her in my arms as one might a new-born baby. With all my new strength, it is as if I am holding a baby in my arms, not a fully grown woman. I use my right arm to help Alex of the floor and he hops up.

"Are you hurt?" I ask.

"I'm fine, just got knocked out during the crash. They rammed us from the side and sent us straight into the wall. Me and Mes jumped out in time. The others weren't so lucky, there was nothing we could do, we had to jump or die Stuart. When I came to, I saw them picking Mes up and I just let off as many shots as I could and they ran off and dropped her."

I don't know why he's trying to explain himself to me, maybe he wants a bit of comfort. I can see the regret in his face, he was in charge of the safety of these people, so he feels responsible for every one of their deaths. He needs someone to tell him that he did the right thing, but it's Alex, I don't want him to lose it now. He's been the strong man since I met him. I need to take his mind of the crash and lives that were lost. He needs to concentrate on helping his sister. He can grieve and blame himself later.

"We need to get her help now. Where's the closest camp?"

"Closest is Halifax but we're not gonna get there in time together without a car. You need to take her, Stuart."

"What ya talking about? Alex, I'm not leaving you here."

"Stuart, she's my little sister. You could reach Halifax in two hours or less with your speed. I'll slow us down and that risks Mes dying. I can't do that. I will be fine. I can handle myself."

I can't leave Alex. If I get Mes to safety and she wakes up fine, she is going to blame me for leaving Alex.

"We've had too many deaths already, Alex. I'm not letting Mes lose her brother when she doesn't have to."

I grab him by his shoulder and throw his arm over mine and set off walking down the street.

"We need to find you a car. Come on quick, they could be anywhere."

He takes his arm off me and walks on his own.

"If you're gonna be a stubborn bastard and stay, I'm ok to walk by myself, mate".

He gives me a little grin which always follows one of his cheeky remarks. It makes me feel a little bit better because it means that grin shows him taking his mind of the situation and then he can be more in control if anything was to turn up. He might still only be human but he knows how to kill lurkers, and the way it's looking we are going to need that. When we set off, there is not going to be a car in sight for miles and the moon is currently at its highest. It's not only the lurkers who attacked the camp who will be roaming the streets tonight, the rest of them will be as well.

"I'm sorry, Stuart," Alex says suddenly, breaking a ten minute silence as we walk and search the streets for a vehicle.

"For what?"

"When I called you a monster and said you are just like the rest of them. I shouldn't have said that."

"You were right though. When you said that to me, I wasn't me and I would have killed you if I was free. I pictured it in my head over and over, I couldn't stop imagining it, so I suppose I should be the one to apologize"

He looks surprised, and comes to a standstill.

"Fuck, really?"

"I couldn't help it. Even when Kimmy came in, I felt like I could have actually killed her as well. Part of me wanted to. The last thing she heard me say was, I will kill you. That wasn't me. I could never hurt her. It was so strange, like there was another person in my body controlling everything I did and I was just sat back watching, not able to stop or take control."

"What brought ya back, then?"

I think back to being in that room and the moment I realized I was fully in control of my own actions again was when I heard Kimmy praying. I felt myself, this self, slowly slip back into control of my own mind and fight the lust for her, not for my own pain.

"Kimmy. I could hear her in her room crying and praying. The fear of losing her gave me the strength to break through the other person, and take control of my emotions again."

"How does it feel? To be one of them, to be able to do the things you can do?"

"I could bite ya and ya could find out?"

I let out a big laugh and Alex joins in and pats on the shoulder.

"I'm not that curious, mate."

We come to the end of the block and we turn and look down the street to the left. Finally, there is a car tipped upside down in the middle of the road. It's a small street with a tall brick wall resulting in a dead end. Each side consists of a row of old stone houses, at least five on each side. There could be anyone inside. We stop for a second at the turning.

"Is there owt down there, Stuart?"

I try to listen for any movement but there is nothing. It must be empty.

“I can't hear anything.” I nod towards the car, “Do ya think it will still work?”

He jogs to it.

“Only one way to find out.”

I follow, jogging up beside him. The car is a small blue Volkswagen Polo. The windows are smashed on each side, dents all over the main body. It looks like lurkers attacked whoever was in the car at the time.

I pass Mes to Alex and grip the edge of the broken window with my fingers. With all my new strength, I pull the car and lift it to its side. I push it the rest of the way. The noise it made as it landed back on its tyres was loud and echoed around the street; if any lurkers was nearby, they would have heard that for sure. I look through the window and everything looks like it’s still together. The car is empty. I can smell blood on the back seat and on the floor under the driver’s seat, but it has no effect on me. The amount of self-control I currently have is unbelievable when only a couple days ago I wanted to tear my friend’s head off to get a small bowl of blood that was driving me insane.

“Do you know how to wire a car?” I ask Alex. If he doesn’t, we are screwed because I have never had to steal a car before and wire it up. The only reason I had the old couple’s car is because the keys were left near the front door. He passes Mes back to me.

“Course I do, mate, look where I grew up!” He lets out a chuckle and jumps into the driver’s seat. I open the passenger door, pull the seat forward and place Mes in the back seat. I’m still surprised how easily I can lift her with just the one arm. I’m interested to see how Alex would wire the car so I head back around to his side to watch. He pulls out the box below the steering wheel which reveals a bunch of wires hanging out, tangled around the metal underneath.

"Do us a favour, mate, and twist the steering wheel til it brakes all the way round," he says, so I listen and grab the wheel but before I could spin it around, he grabs my hand.

"Don't pull the whole wheel off," he warns me. "Just twist it, mate." He gives me a nod, so I spin it gently and it cracks all the way around, breaking all the pins one by one that were keeping it locked. He snaps two of the wires a red and black one, pulls out the copper inside it and sparks them together which only sets off the window wipers. Alex looks confused, which gives me an inkling that he might not be the best at this.

"Oops, wrong wire."

He grabs the green wire and does the same. This time it sparks and the engine tries to start up, stuttering and banging. He keeps sparking them together and suddenly the car springs to life. He sits back and lets out a long breath in relaxation.

"Piece of cake, told you I could do it."

He turns the headlights on and his face suddenly drops and his skin whitens with fear so I look down the street to see six lurkers stood at the end in front of the brick wall, staring at us only about three houses down. I can hear Alex's heart begin to beat much faster. He throws the car into gear but I know he will never get away in time. They are faster than this car and he needs to turn around before he can even begin to hit full speed.

I need to give him time to escape. I could at least hold them off as he turns the car around which would give him and Mes a much larger chance of escape, so I make a quick decision and I step out of the car and slam the door shut.

"Stuart, what the bloody hell ya doing? Get back in the car now!"

"Go Alex. We'll never make it by trying to drive out of here, they'll chase us down. Get Mes out of here and if you see Kimmy..." my mind wonders to her beautiful face and it saddens me that it's unlikely I'll ever see her again, but what would I be if I just let these beasts get a hold of Alex and Mes? I have the ability to do something and I'm going to do it.

"Tell her I'm fine. Tell her that I escaped and I am dealing with this by myself for now. Please don't tell her about this, she doesn't need anything else to worry about."

"Don't do this, Stuart. There's too many of them."

"I have to. You will never make it out alive if I don't, so go!" I snarl as I walk around to the front of the car and Alex does as I say, slamming it into reverse and speeding down the street. I mentally wish him luck. He's on his own now.

A lurker in the middle of the group, a man with short black hair, shining red eyes and a strong jaw signals to a woman beside him with long dark hair with a quick nod. He is clearly in charge. She sets off running towards me. I clench my fists and get my body ready for the fight coming. It's like a natural reaction: my body starts to boil and my strength rises up ready to unleash in battle. It forms an aura of anger around my body and my vision melts into the redness, as if blood has covered my eyes.

I stride forward as fast as I can and slam my hand into her chest which knocks her down to the floor but before I know it another hand has grabbed me and flung me across the street. One against six was never good odds. I twist my body in the air bringing me back to the floor on my feet landing at a squat, sliding across with my hand on the floor to steady myself. My hand glides over brushing the top of a piece of glass probably from the car windows, I grasp it and ready myself for an onslaught of lurkers, but the rest just watch as if enjoying the fight. These are different I can tell. The male lurker who threw me comes running towards me, I swing it at him. It sticks in his ribs, then I throw my left fist around with as much force as I can. I knock him across the road. The woman gets up and dives into my chest, sending us both skidding onto the pavement. She lands on top of me and smashes her hand into my face, crashing my head against the concrete. The pain is unreal, my head feels like it is going to crush into a hundred pieces under her palm. I quickly grab her head with both my hands and twist until I hear her neck snap. I throw her off me, immediately jump up and go to crush her head with my foot, but I get slammed into the side of the house before I can lift my foot. The wall caves in around me. My body gives in and my arms drop to my side, my energy and anger depleted. I look up and the male lurker with short black hair has me by the neck, cutting of the blood rush to my brain. I can feel the power surging from him like a wave. The two lurkers I was fighting stand back up, healed and stand behind him, like bodyguards.

He looks at me for a few seconds so piercingly; it's like he has broken every bone in my body. I force myself to meet his gaze and look him in the eyes, his eyes as red as blood itself. I could see the murder in his eyes, the evil, he wasn't angry and rabid but cold and calculating. It was like looking into the eyes of the devil himself.

"Interesting" he whispers, right before my mind and body give way and I pass out.

Chapter 9

A dripping sound wakes me - water splashing on solid stone floor. The smell of sewage runs up my nostrils, which brings me springing up from the cold damp floor. My vision starts to clear and I see a tap on the side of the wall, dripping water out onto the floor around a small grate in the corner of the room. There are dead rats in that corner. They like someone has squeezed the life out of them. I take a look around the rest of the room. I'm surrounded by brick walls on three sides. There are thick metal bars across the final side, creating a cage, like a prison cell from the movies, but the cage door is open and there is nobody around.

This feels like a trap, but if they already have me and could easily have locked me in, why would they be setting another trap? Where the hell have they brought me anyway? This is obviously a prison cage but the door is wide open for me to walk straight out.

I keep quiet. It's not hard to be quiet anymore, I barely have to think about it and I don't want to alarm anybody and let them know that I am awake. I slowly pad towards the door. To my right are a few more caged rooms and a door at the end of the dingy hall. I am in the final cage, the furthest from the exit. To my left is just a solid wall so there is only one way to go. I walk past the second cage; it is empty. In the third and last cage there is a person in one corner. I can't see his face as he is laid down on his belly on a bed, his head facing the opposite wall. He must be an old man as he has a full head of grey hair matted and scruffy, t shirt and jeans ripped an torn, dry blood stains and dirt, he must have been here a while.

I can't let him out. I can't tell if he is a human or a lurker so I let him sleep and continue to the door. It's big and wooden and it's closed. I can't see through to the other side, but my choice is either to stay here or to try my luck on the other side of the door and staying here does not seem an appealing option.

I push the door open as slowly as I can, creeping out, trying to make the least noise possible. I take a step out and my step takes me onto a soft red carpet, which muffles any sound my foot would have made. I scan the room I have just entered. It's a huge living room with dark oak wainscoting, with old oil portrait paintings adorning the walls. There is a leather sofa in the middle of the room facing a huge brick fireplace, a fire built up and burning on the hearth. This room is amazing; it is nearly as big as the whole cottage Kimmy and I were living in. There are no windows.

Stepping from a line of rat-infested cages into this much luxury seems impossible and I take another look around, shocked. There is a painting above the mantle of a man who resembles the lurker who knocked me out. In the painting, he is stood at the bottom of a staircase in an old-fashioned suit dating to what looks like the eighteenth century. It must be his ancestor or something but the family resemblance is striking - he looks just like him.

There are two doors on either side of the fireplace, both are big wooden doors. I decide to try the closest which is the one on the right-hand side. I try twisting the ornate doorknob but it is locked. I could probably break through it but I don't want to make any noise. If they still think I am asleep, it will be far easier for me to escape. I go to the left door and try to open it. It makes a small click and the door opens up. I gently push it, sneaking through as soon as the gap is wide enough for me to squeeze through. It leads me into an open space. In front of me is a grand staircase with red carpet going all the way up which splits into two other staircases curling around either way to a floor above me. I walk up to it and realise, surreally, that I've just seen this scene before walking into it

- it is the background of the painting I was looking at.

To my left is a big wooden door leading outside. The windows have big red curtains covering them but I can see a little light shining through them. This seems too easy. How could I be at the front door already without anyone stopping me? Without running into anybody? There has to be something else going on here.

But I don't waste any time trying to puzzle it out. If I have the opportunity to leave, I best not waste it. I run straight dart to the door, fling it open and run out into the daylight. I run down the gravel path towards a huge metal gate cutting across the driveway. Just as I go to leap the gate, I feel my body start to heat up. This is the same feeling I get when my body is getting ready for a battle but this time it is on a much larger scale. My body starts to burn to the point that I feel like I am on fire. I look at my arms and can see steam boiling off of them and the skin starting to peel away in layers. The pain becomes too strong and I have to scream and drop to the floor. I turn back towards the house but my eyesight then fails me. My eyes are burning so much that the layers of skin on my eyes have peeled away too, blinding me and causing the house to disappear. I can't see where I am going but I stumble along anyway. The pain is just too unbearable, this time it is going to kill me. I can feel my body melting away so I just start running blindly, hoping for the best, hoping I'm going in the right direction. I suddenly hit a solid wall which nearly knocks me to the ground but the pain of the sun is far worse. I just shake the pain of the impact off and it dissipates. I tentatively use my hands against the wall to feel around, trying to find the door. My body can't take much more. I'm pushing it to the limit. Where is the door? My head gets lighter as I get weaker. If I pass out in this sun, within a matter of minutes, I will be a pile of ash on the floor. I can't die this way, not like this, not now. I need to see Kimmy one more time and tell her everything is going to be fine so that she does not waste time trying to find me and never letting go. I suddenly feel glass instead of stone. I throw myself through the window as fast as I can without a second thought. I go straight through the glass as it shatters around me and fall to the ground. The curtain falls down on top of me in a tangle, blocking the sun from scorching my body. The pain fades unbelievably fast but my body is shaking and fighting to heal itself under the very heavy material weighing me down. I can hear a sizzling coming off my arms and can smell my own flesh like it has been cooked in an oven and served for dinner.

Then I hear the door slam shut and someone laughing.

"Now that was very entertaining."

A male voice, in a very distinguished accent hard to recognise.

My body is still weak, still healing itself but I manage to move my scorched arms and pull the curtain off me. My eyesight begins to come back. The sun is still shining through the broken window but thankfully I am not in its beam and the shade is soothing.

My vision clears up and now I can see the female lurker I was fighting with, her dark hair cascading down. She is very beautiful now that I can see her clearly - bright green eyes, a strong sharp jaw line and cheek bones perfectly lined up. She looks to be in her late twenties so not too much older than me. And she is wearing a well-cut, tight black dress which is modest enough to brush her knees whilst also showing her cleavage to good advantage. Every inch of her, including her poise and self-assuredness, is pure perfection like an art sculpture made of flesh.

The male voice comes from behind me again.

"Seems in your hurry to escape, you forgot one main thing: that you're one of us now, and that means no more sun."

He laughs again, delightedly as he walks slowly down the stairs towards me, clasping his hands together like an amused little boy.

He might be acting like a boy but he is dressed impeccably in an expensive black suit. His short black hair is well-groomed and his skin is as white as paper and his glowing red eyes match the interior of his whole house it seems. The only thing I wasn't expecting was the huge smile on his face. He looks to be middle aged.

"Why did you bring me here?"

I ask not expecting any reasonable answer but in the hope I might find out indirectly what they want with me.

He reaches the bottom off the staircase, drops his smile and gives me a look that frightens me to my very soul. For a second, I am convinced he is about to kill me.

"What's your name?" he asks maintaining this serious look on his face. His accent is so confusing I can't pin point where he is from. It sounds like he's out of his time or so many social spheres above me, which would explain the huge mansion.

"Stuart, Stuart Lister".

His eyes seemed to widen, I would say in recognition if that wasn't nonsensical, but then his face went straight back as if chiselled from marble.

"Well Stuart, this lovely women behind you is Claire, my name is Nathaniel."

He walks over to a set of double doors on the other side of the staircase and swings them open.

“After you.” he says elegantly and pointedly, gesturing me into the room.

Then it dawns on me that I will not be going anywhere any time soon. They have me here until the sun goes down, so there is no point in trying to escape. I might as well amuse them until my opportunity comes to get out of here. Otherwise I might be locked into one of the cells.

I pull myself up from the floor and disentangle myself from the curtain. Claire walks into the room so I follow, walking past Nathaniel who holds open the doors and I enter a room so huge it stops me in my path. The ceiling so high that it would take a thirty-foot ladder to reach it. Red wall paper with thin gold lines running through it coats the whole room. A long wooden table stretches across the room and the far side is adorned with a stone fireplace. Claire walks down the room with a walk that is so proud. Her shoulders remain stiff while her hips swing from side to side. My eyes drop towards her bottom but she glances over her shoulder and catches me looking. She flashes me an alluring smile. I feel guilty for looking but it was just an automatic reaction to this beautiful, rather entrancing woman in front of me.

I feel a hand on the small of my back and push me gently, forcing me to start walking again. Nathaniel now walks alongside me, keeping his hand on my back. At the end of the table is an adjacent room into which we walk, with a black leather sofa with two matching chairs on either side. They all face into the middle of the room, positioned around a gold and red rug on the floor. There is a huge window with the curtains drawn tightly shut and to the right are two men in suits stood on either side of a double door like bodyguards, statuesque with their hands clasped behind their backs, bright red eyes gleaming. Claire seats herself gracefully on the sofa, crossing her legs.

“Take a seat, Stuart,” Nathaniel says.

But there is no way I can get comfortable. I have no idea what is going on or why they have me here. Everything about this is confusing. I never imagined lurkers would live this way; the house is so clean and beautiful in a dark antique way.

Every time I pictured lurkers and where they might live, I imagined them surviving like animals, hiding in caves or dens until the night comes when they leave and explore trying to find whatever food they can.

I never imagined rich families sitting in such ostentatious rooms, having normal conversations with each other. Almost every time I have seen a lurker, their face resembles a savage animal growling with saliva dripping from their fangs, raging with anger. Elegance and decadence were not what I was expecting.

"I would rather stand," I said.

"Suit yourself." He nods to the two lurker guards and they both disappear through the door they appeared to be guarding. They close it behind them.

"Normally I would not bring… hmmm… what is it that the humans have taken to calling us, my dear?"

He asks turning to Claire.

She smiles. "Lurkers," she replies simply.

He lets out a small chuckle, "Yes that's it. Lurkers. Normally, Stuart, I would not bring street lurkers back to my home, but you caught my interest last night."

"What do you mean caught your interest? Your two goons tried to kill me!"

Claire stares right at me. "Goon?" she says witheringly giving me a look as if she wants to tear my head clean off and only her self-restraint is stopping her.

But Nathaniel just laughs, lowering himself into the far chair in front of the huge window. He sits with his elegantly legs crossed and his arms resting perfectly on each chair arm.

"Yes, but that is how you caught my interest. You see I can tell you are only young. You may have begun your new life no more than a week ago, am I right?"

And he is right. I have been a lurker now since the transformation days ago, but I have no idea where he is going with this. What has that got to do with anything?

"I will assume by your silence that I am correct. Now one as young as yourself should not have been able to let a human drive away from you so easily, let alone risk your own life to help him escape. And I won't forget that you could have destroyed Claire if I…" He enjoys a little pause as he smiles at Claire. "Well if I had not intervened."

"That human you are speaking about was my friend. That's why I can help him and not feed on him like you monsters would have."

I really should not keep insulting these people but everything about this situation is driving me insane. It's an impulse reaction I can't control. My anger is always there, ready to explode, trying to escape and take over my actions.

"We are not monsters, Stuart. We simply eat the food we are designed to eat. We are the higher species in this world. Would you call a butcher a monster for slaughtering a pig? We do what we must."

He rises from his armchair and walks towards me slowly. The door swings open and the two bodyguards come walking through dragging what looks like the man from the prison room. His head is down so I still cannot see his face. They drag him up to my side and they drop him on his knees. Nathaniel who is now right in front of me.

"What's going on?"

I really don't like the look of this situation. This man they have brought through is clearly a human now I can see him better. He is weak, sweaty and I can smell the blood leaking from his wounds and the scratches across his arms. His heartbeat is so weak that he is barely alive. I can only imagine what hell they have been putting this poor man through, torturing him and teasing him like a poor defenceless animal in a cage.

"I said I was interested in you Stuart. Your strength is very valuable to me as well as your knowledge; I need people like you to join my army. The humans have become stronger and wiser so we must expand and do the same. I own the northern side."

His voice gets stronger and more serious. I can see the conversation is taking a horrible twist. "And if my brothers in the south were to get wind of the trouble that these northern rebellions including your little group have given me, not only my honour but my leadership would be challenged. And I refuse to be embarrassed in that way."

He grabs the man by his head and pulls his face up. I can't believe my eyes. The shock of seeing this person on the floor, beaten and weak, in this state causes me to take a step back almost dropping into the chair behind me. It's Mr Fisher, Tommy, Kimmy's dad. He's captured here and beaten half to death. How is he in front of me? He was supposed to be in Halifax safe, waiting for Kimmy. It looks like they have had him for more than one night. They could not have caught him last night during the attack, but if they did, does that mean they could have Kimmy too? What if they caught up with their truck further down the road after attacking Alex and Mes'?

Tommy looks up at me. His eyes widen and his face changes from expressing his exhaustion and weakness to be overwhelmed with pure fear as he recognises me. He opens his mouth, "Stuart?" he croaks with what energy he has left.

I still can't believe my eyes. I am stuck for words. I can't even open my mouth. I just stare at him, half in denial that he is here.

He scrambles to his feet and leaps for me with what strength he has left, screaming, "You traitorous piece of shit!"

But Claire drags him back down before he can get anywhere.

"Aah so you know this piece of meat, don't you, Stuart?"

Tears drop from Tommy's face, his anger faded away in his desperation. "Stuart, where's Kimmy? Don't tell me she's gone. Please don't tell me she's gone."

I try to answer his question to tell him she's fine, that she escaped, but before I can, Nathaniel throws his head back down knocking him to the ground at my feet. Nathaniel speaks before I can.

"Now this particular human has killed more of my men then I would like to count. And, despite our efforts, he is still unwilling to give me any information about his people's location. Humans and their love for one another… it's pathetic."

I finally manage to open my mouth and get out a few words.

"What are you gonna do with him?"

Nathaniel starts to laugh and takes Claire by the hand and brings her to her feet from the sofa. He winds his arm around her waist and they both smile at me. There is no comfort in these smiles - they are dark and mischievous. There is nothing happy inside their smiles.

"This is my favourite part," Claire says to Nathaniel. He kisses her on the forehead and she steps away to the side. The two bodyguards retreat back to the door but this time they block it, preventing anyone escaping. Clearly, the situation is about to get a lot worse. Everything about this is ominous and is making me tense.

"*We* are not going to do anything, Stuart. We need you to help us. You know the group. You know where they are, do you not? Well to be with us, you will need to use your natural instincts. You need to become the same as us and stop ignoring what you truly are. So prove it and kill him."

They want me to feed on Tommy, on my girlfriend's dad. This is insane. What are they thinking?

"You must be insane if you think I am going to kill him, if you think I am ever going to join you."

There is an underlying anger in his voice when he replies.

"Why not? Because you have a lingering respect for them? You need to wake up, Stuart. Stop holding on to what you used to be and allow yourself to become so much more."

"I will not kill him!" I shout.

"Why not? Because you believe you are still one of them?"

"I am one of them!"

"Wake up, you fool. You are one of us."

"I will never be one of you."

I don't know if it's just frustration causing my actions, I feel so trapped, or desire to show Tommy that I'm not a traitor but I swing towards Nathaniel throwing my fist towards him. Before I can get near him, he grabs my hand and twists his arm around my neck and throws me towards the mirror, holding onto my head with his other arm. I should have known I could not overpower him.

"Do you think that they will accept you now? It does not matter how hard you try to fight what you are, they will always see a monster. Look in the mirror, Stuart, LOOK!" He shouts with an intensity which makes my body shake.

My eyes automatically go towards the mirror and once again I see my eyes shining, but this time I look different. My skin has turned pale white as if I have never seen the light of day, my fangs are now fully grown, jutting past my lips and sharp as daggers. The sight of myself forces me to close my eyes. It is unbearable. I felt something sliding down my cheek so I re-open my eyes to find a small tear of blood from my right eye more black than red leaking down my face and leaving a streak behind. How could I face Kimmy looking like this? Nathaniel was right. How could they accept me when I am one of the beasts that have ruined the world and killed so many of their loved ones?

Nathaniel whispers in my ear, "See what you really are and just accept it, Stuart." He speaks softly and enticingly. I wonder whether his voice has ever not worked to entrance someone before. It's not working on me. He continues, "You will have a new family here. You will never grow old. Stuart, you will never get ill and you can have whatever your mind desires. And all you need to do is let go of the past and embrace your new life."

I shrug Nathaniel's arms off me and collapse into the chair. The only thought on my mind is never being able to see Kimmy again. She is the only person I desire, the only one thing that gives my life meaning in this new crappy world. Everything else is just water under the bridge. I could learn to live as a lurker, but the thought of never seeing her again brings me more pain than I am able to handle. But then again, maybe Kimmy would be better off never seeing me again, like this, to believe I was dead. Then she could move on and have as normal a life as she can in the camps, a life without me.

Mr Fisher begins coughing, trying to catch his breath which brings me back to the room and out of my thoughts. I scan the room, all eyes are on me awaiting my decision but patiently. These people are not in a rush. They have all the time in the world for me to come to terms with what I am. They understand it takes time. I need to use that to figure out a plan of action. I almost forgot about Mr Fisher and what they expect me to do to him, but it's an easy decision: I would never hurt anybody like that. My features and physical strength may have changed but I am still me, my mind is still my own. A sudden rush of exhilaration runs through my body as I realise Kimmy was right back in that room. She insisted that I would have a choice, that once I changed I would still be me. The man in the station had done it and so have I. She knew that, and she will always see me as the man who she fell in love with. I cannot give in to these beasts. Even if I look like a monster, it does not mean that I am one. I cannot give up on Kimmy so I need to get myself and Mr Fisher out of here. Nathaniel is too strong to fight my way past and there seem to be too many guards around the house. I need to pretend; I need to make them believe… I must make them believe that I have no other choice but to stay with them. I also need them to keep Mr Fisher alive long enough to free him.

The intensity of the room comes back to me and I see the creases on Nathaniel's head begin to grow as his evil red eyes darken. He might be patient but that patience can still wear thin. Looking at him is like staring into an empty soulless pit. He won't wait much longer for my decision.

I stand up as stiffly as I can, keeping my eyes fixed on Nathaniel's red soulless eyes gleaming back at me in confusion.

“You are right, Nathaniel. They could never accept me for what I am now. If I go back, they’ll ostracise me. So, I can’t go back.”

His eyes widen and his smile grows so large it takes over his face. A laugh follows, but I wouldn’t call it a cheerful laugh. It’s sinister, a dark laugh of accomplishment and power. He clasps his hands together and comes towards me. I try not to flinch.

“Excellent, Stuart, just, excellent. You have made a wise choice my young friend.”

He threw his arms around my shoulders and walked me towards the door where the guards still stand.

“What about him?” I ask pointedly looking towards Mr Fisher, trying to be emotionless but I cannot leave the room thinking that they will kill him as soon as I am gone.

Nathaniel looks at Mr Fisher then at Claire, who responds with a deviant smile.

“What do you think we should do with him, Stuart?” he replies. Here it is, my first test to see if I am truly on their side. Once again, the room becomes silent, the tension rises and eyes stalk me as I make my decision.

“If he’s one of their prize fighters, wouldn’t killing him be too easy? They must need him. Why don’t we keep him as leverage?”

He gives me a long intense look, “Indeed,” he replies. He loses interest quickly in Mr Fisher. “Take him back to his cage,” he tells the guards lazily. They grab

Tommy and force him out of the room, which isn't hard given how weak he is.

A weight drops from my shoulders, knowing he is safe for now, but not for long given the mess he is in.

Nathaniel's attention then turns fully onto me. We talk, and I am very careful with my answers, and he shows me around his house. It is built like a maze, corridors twist and turn and each endless hall leads to room after room, all lined with the same deep red carpet and gold and red wall paper. The whole set up freaks me out. I think he likes red a bit too much. Eventually, we reach the room he has assigned me. I've never stayed somewhere so fancy. There is a big old oak bed in the centre and what looks like a balcony behind the window but, as with every other window, the light is blocked out with huge heavy red curtains. By the time we reach the room, my body is tired and weak. Nathaniel explains that we lose our strength during the day and without sleep our bodies begin to shut down, our minds clear and the thirst takes over us, clouding our judgement and taking away our own will.

My plan had been to grab Mr Fisher and wait by the door until the sun went down, whilst the rest were asleep in their own rooms and then to run as far as possible. But as soon as I lie on the bed, my body sinks into the mattress, and I am more comfortable than I've ever been in my life. It isn't long before my eyes shut and suddenly I wake up abruptly to find the sun has gone, the curtains pure darkness, no sunlight hitting from behind. There is a new smell in the room. It's odd but it is a familiar smell to me, cigar smoke and whisky, but I can't place why it is familiar. It is comforting though. It brings me out of my sleep state and I notice a figure in the corner of the room.

In a split second I have jumped out of the bed, sending the quilt flying from my unbelievable new strength and speed. For the first time, a thought wells up from the back of my brain thinking that I could get used to this. My new skills are rather brilliant. But I tamper the thought as I have something more pressing to address. The man stands still in the corner looking at me as I scan him. He is short, maybe about 5 foot 8 inches or so with short brown hair brushed forward and he does not look threatening despite being clearly a lurker. He's dressed simply in dark chinos and a brown cotton jumper. I should be scared, but I'm not. It's something in his eyes, I think. They are not evil - they shine bright brown, the same colour as mine, and the look on his face is calm. The whole scene seems unreal.

"am I dreaming?" I say out loud mainly to myself. As the scene feels unreal.

But he answers in a low calm, comforting voice, "No, Stuart, you are not dreaming."

He steps forward, standing no further than a metre from me. Then I realise I recognise him. The man in front of me is the lurker who we saw on the camera back during our first night in the camp. But before I could compute this or say a word, he interrupts my thoughts: "You have to leave this place, Stuart. This is not for you." His expression seems almost as if he is pained to see me here.

"What? Who are you? What are you doing here?" The stream of questions escapes me as my mouth catches up with my baffled brain.

"I can't believe I allowed this to happen to you. Please leave here as soon as possible," he pleads.

My frustration rises. Who is this mysterious man? How has he allowed anything to happen to me as if he is in control when I do not have the slightest idea of who he is.

"Look, you can't just show up and say this to me without explaining. Who are you? What do you want?"

“There will be time for that, but the night is here. Come with me now before Nathaniel wakes up. I can help you, Stuart.”

“How do you know my name?”

“I know more about you than you know, but there's a war going on, you should not be here.”

“Don't you think I know that? I don't want to be here! I am not going to help them win the war against the rebellion.”

“Not the rebellions you are thinking of, Stuart.”

“What? Who then?”

“There are others like us.”

The door swings open and my eyes dart across to see who it is. Claire stands in the doorway with two guards, not honouring me with a knock. “Ah, you’re awake good,” she drawls with her long drawn out vowels. I turn back to the man but he has gone and the smell with him.

As I am left confused by the mystery man, Claire strolls up to me.

“Everything okay, Stuart?” she asks with not the smallest amount of care in her voice. She’s caught me off-guard and I snap more than I should, given that I am in their power. “Yes I am fine. What do you want?”

“Now Stuart,” she responds patronisingly, “don't be so rude. Nathaniel would like you to join him for breakfast.” She walks towards the balcony and closes the open door letting in the wind which was blowing the curtains ever so slightly.

Breakfast. I hate to think what they mean by breakfast. The horrible silent walk through the halls with Claire and the guards is utter torture. The worst thing is my awareness of this beautiful, seductive woman next to me. She's so close and the smell of her is setting off a chemical reaction in my body. I have to fight my urges and her low-cut dress, hugging her figure is not helping. In my human days, this would have been an easy urge to resist but, as a lurker, every one of my senses are heightened, including my sex drive is going crazy. I try not to watch her tight bottom as her hips sway from side to side. Vivid images of flinging her against the wall and taking her rise unbidden into the forefront of my brain and are difficult to shift. The danger, her lack of interest in me and how easily she would find it to knock me down all only heighten the feelings. I try to think of Kimmy and focus on the betrayal it would be towards her and this keeps me marginally calm but my mind continues to cheat on her.

Distraction comes from another avenue. I think back to what the short lurker said before Claire burst into my room. There are others like us. What did he mean by this? All lurkers? Or me and him in general? Who was this mystery man? His sudden appearance gives me the inkling that there might be something going on much bigger than what we have imagined so far. He clearly is not in league with Nathaniel but knows how to disappear within his house. I do not have time to think about it further as we reach the huge dining room and there is Nathaniel seated at the end of the table in the huge master's chair. All desire for Claire and thoughts of my guest flee my mind.

"Ah, Stuart. Take a seat, my new friend." I try to seat myself as far away as possible, choosing the first seat I come to but he gestures me towards the chair at his right hand.

"You must be starving." He clicks his fingers and the far door bursts open as two guards, one male, one female enter, dragging a young woman hog-tied and gagged, almost causing me to leap out of my seat in horror. The innocent woman screams furiously, trying to escape, throwing her body in every direction possible to break free. It's horrible to watch and not help. The poor woman knows what is coming; I can see it in her eyes as they throw her down to her knees by Nathaniel's chair. Her breathing is heavy and I can hear her heart beating a mile a minute. Tears stream down her face; her eyes are so wide that the red veins bulge out showing her fear, her upmost fear. It is enough to make me cry, but I have to keep strong. I can't give Nathaniel any reason not to trust me.

None of this fazes Nathaniel a bit. He grabs her by the jaw and moves her head back and forth scanning both sides of her neck, his eyes wide pin-pointing every vein and artery.

"So precious and innocent. This one will be perfect," he says aloud. I force myself to keep looking. Then he turns to me with a smile which makes my heart stop and my skin crawl. I know what is coming and I can't stop it. The woman looks right at me too, screaming and sobbing for help. What can I do? The room is full of lurkers. I would be dead before I could even reach her. I want to help her with every fibre in my body. My heart screams to do something, do something now, say something, just try something.

Then it is too late. She is gone.

Chapter 10

Richard stands in a dark room. He is not alone. Suddenly, he hears footsteps coming closer, the sound of three maybe four people. The door swings open and with one swift move he is out of the balcony doors and leaping onto the grass in the back garden, landing perfectly on his feet after a two-story drop. The sound of a woman's voice comes closer to the balcony. He throws himself up against the wall directly underneath to stay hidden. The door slowly closes.

He drops his head with a sense of failure then makes his way around the house. A male guard stands at one corner of the house so Richard waits for him to turn away before racing around it. He subdues the man by breaking his neck and laying him down gently on the ground this should keep him down for abit. He walks up to a window where the light is shining out and suddenly hears screams, female screams. When he peers in, he sees Nathaniel holding a tied-up woman on the floor beside him. Then he looks at the other man in the room who has a terrified look on his face and sympathy runs through his whole body for the boy, for his son. As much as he would love to run in and decapitate Nathaniel and save both the innocent woman and his boy, there is nothing he can do to help them now. He just hopes that Stuart survives long enough for him to help. There is no hope for the girl. She has mere minutes left to live, if that. No point him watching, so he sets off running and leaps over the giant walls surrounding the grounds.

He runs through the gardens, ducking and diving to hide from other lurkers who are searching the streets as he does not want to get into any bother with the local suckers, random lurkers with no home or allegiances. They do as they do. They are not much bother to him - he has bigger fish to fry. He finally reaches an alley between two large buildings and bangs on a huge metal door. A metal plate between the door slides open and two shining eyes peer at him for a few seconds. The door swings open and a huge lurker greets him with a smile.

“Ah Richard, you’re back.” Richard shakes the lurker’s hand and enters.

“Good to see you again, my friend,” he replies. He takes a turn and walks down some stairs and through another door where dozens of lurkers are relaxing in a huge room, playing pool, drinking beer, talking and giggling. As he walks through, he is greeted by several of them. He is clearly well-known and well-liked here. Eventually, he reaches another room where a woman who looks to be a similar age as him and with long brown hair, green eyes, a strong jaw jumps to her feet.

“Richard, my god, I wasn't expecting you.” She walks over and hugs him.

“Sarah. It’s good to see you again.”

“Take a seat, please. Where have you been?”

“I am sorry Sarah but I am not here for pleasantries. I need your help.”

Sarah looks confused but she obliges regardless. “You need help? Of course. Anything.”

“Nathaniel has someone held captive at his home. I need to get him out before it’s too late.”

She stands up and takes a slow walk over to a bar, grabs a bottle of old malt whisky and pours them both a glass. “This is still your drink I assume?”

“Course. What else?” he replies with a huge smile before taking a mouthful, relishing the taste and enjoying the sensation as it warms his throat and stomach.

“This person, the one Nathaniel has, who is it?”

“He's...” Richard swallows air not whisky this time before replying, “my son.”

The eyes of everyone in the room shoot towards Richard with shock. They can all hear perfectly despite the distance. Sarah places her drink on the table, and leans closer to him.

“You have a son? How do I not know this?”

Richard’s voice becomes tense and has undertones of anger as he replies, “He wasn't a part of this world and I wanted to keep it that way. But this past year it’s become impossible to do so, and now after a series of unfortunate events, he's stuck in Nathaniel's mansion. If he stays there any longer, he won't be the same. You know what Nathaniel will do to him, you know that more than anyone, Sarah. I can't let him take my son away as well.”

The woman stands and paces around the room, thinking hard. “We have plans to take the mansion in a few weeks Richard.”

He jumps to his feet. “A few weeks will be too late. He will be one of them by tomorrow night. You know how persuasive Nathaniel can be. Please. We need to go tonight.”

She walks towards Richard and puts an arm around his shoulders gently. “You are a pain in my arse. Lucky for you, my heart will always have a soft spot for you. Sure, we will go get your son tonight. It’s not going to be easy, mind you. But with you with us, that will be a major help”.

“I know it won’t be. But we can do it. Thank you, Sarah, sincerely. I owe you everything.”

Chapter 11

My mind is engraved with the scene of Nathaniel and Claire using that poor lass like she was a box of wine. It plays on a reel over and over. The screams and images are imprinted on my mind, a real-life horror film happening right in front of me. I'm most horrified by their smiles and the obvious pleasure they got from doing something so repulsive to someone so innocent. This place is hell. If that was breakfast, what is lunch and whatever else they do around here going to be like? I had to take my mind back to the old days when it was just Kimmy and I sat in our comfortable little cottage, eating her rabbit stew and just happy in each other's company. I miss her so much, her soft touch, her beautiful smile that can bring joy to anyone, her gentle voice which calms me in any situation. I miss her so much. Thinking of her was the only thing that kept me from bursting out in the middle of their horror scene of a breakfast.

"I am quite offended that you refused my hospitality earlier, Stuart. Are you having second thoughts?"

I snap back into reality and to the eyes of Nathaniel, currently focused on me but also glazed with pleasure of a full stomach. They have taken the drained corpse out of the room which I am thankful for. The longer she was there, the sicker I felt. A lifeless bloody body is not the ideal thing to be staring at first thing when you wake up. One minute she was there, screaming to me for help, the next she is lying on the floor, lifeless, nothing going through her mind or rushing through her body, just gone. The thought sends a shiver down my spine.

"No," I finally manage to get words to leave my mouth. "It's just… all a bit new to me. I need some time to adjust."

"Then time you shall have," he graciously acceded, taking that terrible gaze off me.

Time… time is not what I need. What I need is to get as far away as possible from these nut jobs. I am stuck here with these psychos with superhuman strength. They are far worse than the rabid street lurkers who just rummage the streets. Those lurkers are reckless and stupid and obeying their animal instincts and bloodlust. These monsters, these are organised. Nathaniel spoke of his army. He has an army and therefore they can do whatever they wish. God knows what their master plan is. They did not bring about this apocalyptic war zone for nothing. There is something much bigger going on here than I imagined and I definitely do not want to be a part of it.

Another man enters the room and quickly whispers in Nathaniel's ear. His face suddenly drops in shock which was the most emotion I had yet seen on him except for that cruel smile which never reached his eyes. Then he stands up, reaching out a hand to Claire who takes it and elegantly lifts herself to her feet.

"My apologies, Stuart, there is a matter that we must tend to. Please make yourself at home." I have to hand it to them, they might be monsters and total nut jobs but they have the best manners I have ever encountered. "And please take some time to adjust, like you said. Tomorrow, we will have the pleasure of showing you what we have in store for the humans. I think you will be quite surprised," he says with a tilted smile on his face. I do not like the sound of that, nor the smile he sends my way as he leaves. I am sure that I am not going to like the sort of surprise that he enjoys. After they leave, I wonder why they are so trusting of me. I have only just got here and I have not given them any reason to trust me yet. But who am I to question? Now might be my moment to grab Mr Fisher and get the hell out of here.

I wait for the voices to fade on the other side of the door, nod politely to the guards, then make my way to the front of the house and through the door at the bottom of the staircase as fast as I possibly can. After slamming the door behind me and spinning round to where the prison corridor is, I am stopped in my tracks by a guard at the door. I wasn't expecting anybody to be guarding him. What did they expect from a halfdead beaten up man? He wasn't about to get up and walk out in his state.

The guard shoots up from the stool he is perched on and analyses me with his eyes. My heartrate rises and my muscles stiffen with the tension in the air.

"What are you doing here?" he asks in a low and confused voice. His face scrunches up when nothing comes out of my mouth.

"You are not supposed to be here," he snarls at me, stepping closer which causes me to edge up against the door. But I need to get Mr Fisher out of here. It is now or never - he clearly can't handle many more beatings. I form a fist and lunge towards the guard with a right hook connecting with his jaw line. The sudden sound of a crunch and the guard drops down to the floor, skidding up to the wall. But with less than a moment to think about my next move, he is already on his feet and throws his stool which hits my face, blinding me. Then he has pounced on me like an animal. He lands on top of me with his hands around my neck. With all the blood rushing to my head raising the pressure inside, I crash my arm down onto the stool breaking it into pieces and I ram a broken piece into his chest forcing him off me. He growls like an injured lion. I quickly snap his neck to keep any other guards from hearing him.

After taking a few moments to catch my breath and composure, I hurry into the prison itself and stop to see Mr Fisher laid on his back, barely breathing, covered in a mixture of dirt, blood, and sweat . The smell is horrendous as it lingers and oxidises in the horribly damp musky room. I yank open the locked cage door as easy as opening a fridge. Once again, my mind is shocked by how unreal my new strength is, but not for long, the horrific sight of Mr Fisher pains me. I cradle my arm around him, bringing him to his feet.

"Stuart," he murmurs gently through the swollen thing that is his face, lumps, bumps and bruises everywhere.

"I'm getting you out of here, Mr Fisher," I tell him softly.

I try to set off walking with him out of the cage but his body flings around like a rag doll, not one of his muscles seem to be working. I have no option but to fling him over my shoulder and carry him out of here.

I make my way to the front door as quickly as I possibly can. We are almost there when I suddenly hear a "STOP." I turn around slowly to see a number of guards stood at the bottom of the huge staircase, all red eyes gleaming and fixed on me.

"I knew Nathaniel was a fool to trust you." A voice rises from the other side of the wall of guards. Claire comes walking through them. "Did you really think I was going to let you just walk out of here so easily? I knew you couldn't join us. You are weak, pathetic, trying desperately to cling onto the last remnant of humanity you possess. Nathaniel believes most people would be too stupid to try betray him, but you're not most people, are you Stuart? You aren't going anywhere. I am going to make you watch as I drain what's left of your friend and then I am going to get rid of you before you can become a nuisance to the cause. You already know too much in my opinion."

There is no way that I am going to escape by simply running. Fighting seems equally pointless but I will not give in so easily. I place Mr Fisher gently down next to the front door and ready myself once again for what is about to come.

"Stupid child. You might have gotten lucky with me last time, but do not make the mistake of thinking we are equals."

"Equal? We are far from equal," I lash out. "You're a monster, an animal, nothing more than a starved beast! At least I still care. I still feel, unlike you and your empty soul."

She lets out a small derisive chuckle.

"And that is why you will not survive, boy. Emotions, pathetic little feelings which linger in you, they make you weak like the humans."

But as the room goes quiet, the floor gently begins to rumble very faintly. It is faint but it is definitely there. The sound grows and the rumbles get heavier as whatever it is nears. The only thing I can think of which might sound similar is a stampede. It gets louder and louder as whatever it is comes closer. Then suddenly, windows begin to smash around the mansion, screams echo around the halls. The guards shoot off to investigate which leaves Claire standing alone, confused and panicked. I reach for Mr Fisher and throw him over my shoulder again. Claire stares me down, but I just turn and sprint out of the front door, knowing she has other problems now and I'm not sticking around to see what is happening. I can't imagine it is good but if it gives me a chance to escape, I'll take it. I level the front gate with a boot which flings it wide open and the whole gate judders from my strength as it threatens to split in two. I sprint away into the night.

I run until the screams and roars from the mansion no longer echo in the streets. I have no idea where I am but I have a destination in mind, the same place where Alex and I were heading the night Nathaniel grabbed me. I have to make my way to Halifax, find the camp and get Mr Fisher some immediate medical care.

Every now and again, I can hear noises in the distance. It's more than likely other lurkers, who can probably smell the blood on Mr Fisher. By the time they realise where the smell is coming from, we will be long gone. My pace never slows and I don't get breathless. Like a machine, I just keep going, street after street, town after town. I stay clear of fields as they are likely to be a feeding ground for the street lurkers, taking down cows or sheep or whatever they could get their hands on when they can't get humans.

Suddenly Mr Fisher, who has been quiet all this time and as light as a pillow, starts to cough and splutter, bringing him out of his comatose sleep. He is still barely able to move so I lie him down against a wall. He raises his head and looks at me with what can only be described as fear. This was something I never thought I would see in this man's face.

"Stuart." He struggles to say my name and fight through the pain of talking. His voice sounds very dry. "What have they done to you?" My head falls with shame when I remember the beast I must look like to him. "Kimmy, where is she?"

"Safe," I say, hoping the words are still true. "She is with John from the Rotherham camp. They were heading to Halifax last time I saw them. And I charged him to look after her." A small smile appears on his face before he can't hold it and drops his head to his chest again. As I go to lift him again, he tries to fight back away from me. "Wait, wait, you are one of them, aren't you? How are you still you?"

"I don't know, just am." And I explain everything to him as he rests. I start at the beginning, when the bombs fell and then, the cabin, the lurker that bit me and the one in the petrol station, everything. He will not let me move him until he knows how his daughter has been since he last heard from her. Even at death's door, he still only worries about his family, not himself. That's the Tommy Fisher I know.

After a while, his body gives up again and he passes out. I once again set off carrying him. But as I'm crossing through this town, I catch the hint of a trickle of water downwind. I shift Mr Fisher so I can look at him properly. He can clearly use a drink. His tongue resembles a rough sponge. Peering through the trees, I cannot catch a scent or noise of another lurker, so I decide to take Mr Fisher down for a rest and to clean him up. I crawl through the trees out into the open field. The further I get the more I realise that it's not a field at all. It's been such a long time since we've had a normal life it takes me a little time to place where I am. As I pass sand pits and flags poked into small holes on neatly grazed grass, I realise it is a golf course. Golf seems like a pastime of another world. Following the small running river through the course, I find a small wooden bridge where we can reach the water without having to jump in. I place him down on the bridge. The night seems so calm; there's not a single noise other than the gentle breeze flowing over the pitch. But it all seems too quiet, making me cautious of the situation. I scan the trees trying to catch any other movement around. And suddenly a small flicker of light inches from the floor catches my eye forcing me to spring backwards, and after my eyes adjust, I see the outline of a person laid on the floor, pinpointing something at me. Before I can recognise it, I hear a click and it is too late. The huge sniper rifle was pointing straight at me and the bullet leaves the chamber and strikes me in the chest, lifting me off my feet and into the river in an instant. I try to catch any breath but my lungs fill up with blood and water and my body gives way. Looking up at the stars as my vision begins to fade, I see Mr Fisher crawl to the end of the bridge and reach for me but it's too late.

Chapter 12

The night is at its zenith. In the darkness, dozens of lurkers sprint through the streets, making their way to the mansion perched at the top of the hill. There are a few familiar faces in the crowd. Richard paces at an inhuman speed at Sarah's side, leading the way. Both have a similar look of determination on their faces. Just before they reach the walls of the huge mansion, they exchange a look which shows anyone watching that they care for each other and they want each other to make it through this assault unharmed. After scaling the wall, the crowd split into packs around the house and, without a pause or any seeming leader giving the direction, each group simultaneously dives like a spear through the old antique windows. Richard throws himself through the window he had been peering through just a few hours before into the dining room, still hoping that his son would still be in there to make this a quick and easy rescue. Three lurkers dive through after him, following him as steadily as bodyguards assigned to protect him would. He scans the room but it is clearly empty. Not so easy then. He heads to the door to search the house but before he can reach it, the far door bursts open and three tall lurkers in suits spot

Richard and the others at the other end of the room. They waste no time racing towards each other, meeting in the middle of the room. Richard flings himself towards one of the suited lurkers, knocking them to the floor with such force that they both skid across the floor to the far door. Richard overpowers the other lurker as he lands on top of them and uses his palm to crush their face. Then, he picks the lurker off the floor and throws him into the wall causing it to crack then throws them again across the room, over the long table and into the huge fireplace on the opposite side of the room. He wastes no time but races towards the lurker, and before they can regain consciousness, he grabs the fire poker and finishes the job, stabbing the head and the heart of one, then grabs the other by the head and pulls, the tearing of his skin screams out with his voice as his head slowly tears off from his shoulders. He quickly turns his attention to the other lurkers who have taken the suits down and are tearing them apart limb by limb.

Leaving them to their duty, he leaves the dining room and makes his way through the mansion to the front where he is stopped in his tracks by the beautiful but monstress lurker, Claire. He's met her before, he knows her well, and he is wary. She is stood unthreateningly enough at the bottom of the staircase with a look of confusion on her face, for once showing her not to be reticent and in control. The confusion clears instantly when she spots Richard.

She lets out a laugh which does not sufficiently cover up the small amount of fear manifested by the attack.

"Richard I should have known."

"Where is he, Claire?"

"You know you really are a bleeding nuisance, Richard." He refuses to be taken in by her games and grabs her by the throat, throwing her up against the wall.

"Ohhh, you remembered I like it rough. How sweet."

"ENOUGH, Claire! Where is he?"

"Nathaniel? He's not in right now, he's already playing out. If you come back in a few hours he might be back then."

"ENOUGH!" he shouts again, this time anger breaks through his voice, frustrated by her games.

"Not Nathaniel." he spits out. "Although he will get his soon enough."

She breaks into laughter.

"Oh, Richard it makes me laugh how you and your pathetic group of emotion-fuelled followers think you can stand up to someone as great and powerful as Nathaniel. You are a baby compared to him."

"Well this baby and his friends have taken over his beloved headquarters and have you by the neck, literally." He says this with a smile on his face, looking to where his hand is wrapped around Claire's neck.

"Now, answer me. Where is Stuart?"

Her eyes widen with surprise as she registers what he has just asked.

"Stuart? What do you have to do with that idiot? Apart from the fact that you both are a pain the arse, of course?"

"None of your business. Now for the last time, where the hell is he?"

"You're a bit too late, Richard. Your little friend already took off, little nuisance that he is, he took the bleeding prisoner with him as well."

Richard looks towards the door. It is wide open. He thinks quickly and decided to believe that she is telling the truth. She would have no reason to lie, if he was there, they would eventually find him after they take the mansion.

"Doesn't matter. Nathaniel has plans for that one. He won't last where he is going. I am sure he will cross our tracks again and I'll be sure to give him hell when he does. I am looking forward to it already."

Richards face drops for fear for his son. It shows so clearly on his face that Claire can see he has an attachment to Stuart greater than friendship. She connects the dots and begins to laugh. "Ooooh, this is marvellous! The self-righteous Richard has a child! Wait until Nathaniel hears about this. We will have a field day on that little offspring of yours."

Richard tightens his grip around Claire's throat to cut off her words.

"I think you are mistaken Claire. What makes you think you are leaving this house? Look at this face. It's going to be the last face you ever see."

He raises his hand and smiles, ready to attack but a scream from the top of the staircase distracts him, long enough for Claire to weasel out of his grip and throw him across the room. She escapes through the open door. By the time he gets back to his feet, it's too late. She is already too far to chase down.

Sarah comes walking down the stairs, dragging one of Nathaniel's disciples behind her who she throws to Richard's feet.

"Tell him what you told me," she demands. "Now!"

The injured lurker looks up at Richard. "We have been herding the humans."

Richard's face drops in confusion and grabs the lurker by the collar and raises him up.

"What do you mean herding humans? Why?"

“Why do you think? They are our food; we eat them. After the war started, they were dropping too fast. The way things were going we would have run out of healthy humans to feed on in a matter of years. So we began to herd them like the cattle they are and breed them in camps all over the world. This way we will have an endless supply.”

He looks into Richard’s eyes, and anger fumes roll off him almost perceptibly.

“The rebellions are the best choice for cattle. They keep themselves fed and healthy, and before long, that idiot of a boy is going to lead us straight to the biggest camp around. There will be hundreds of helpless humans ripe for the taking.”

He starts to laugh in Richard’s face uncontrollably. Sarah suddenly rams a broken piece of wood through the lurker’s chest and Richard drops him to the floor.

“What are we going to do Sarah” Richards asks Sarah urgently, then a friendly lurker comes rushing around the corner, “The mansion is ours, but there's no sign of Nathaniel anywhere.”

“this is your rescue mission Richard, what do you want to do”?

Richard looks at both of them, figuring out what needs to be done. Then jumps straight into command as Sarah allows it.

“I need to find my son fast. I will track his scent and hopefully stop him before he reaches the camp. Sarah, maybe you should take a few of your best men, and find out where this herding is happening. It’s not right. Innocent humans don't deserve this; the world has already become too bad, we don't need more evil. “right!” says Sarah, “Thomas, you keep this place locked down, bring in more fighters. This is a victory we need to keep. Having the mansion gives us an edge in this war."

They all nod to each other in agreement, seeing the sense in Richard's plan. Then they split up, into action.

Chapter 13

Suddenly springing to life, taking a huge gasp of air, my mind instantly snaps into action. Where am I? What happened? I scan the room. This does not take long, it's another four-wall metal container. It is so constricted in width, I can barely spread my legs out full length. There is a metal door with a small latch at head height for the average man. Then the memories come flashing back. The bullet tearing into my chest; Mr Fisher reaching out for me; the river; the golf course. We were attacked. Where is Mr Fisher? Why is he not lying in here with me? Did he not make it? Or is he simply in a different cell?

I easily raise myself to my feet without any struggle. There is no pain left from where the bullet pierced me. My new body does not feel so much pain anymore. There are not any lingering after-effects either. Again, I think there are some advantages to this new state of being. Closing my eyes, I tune into my sensitive hearing. I begin to hear very quiet noises gradually becoming clearer. There is the sound of another door close by scraping open. But I cannot hear a word of speech. It is followed by another door scraping open and then footsteps nearing until they stop right in front of my cell door. I ready myself for what is to come. I have no idea who is on the other side of this door. I'm terrified it might be Nathaniel? Did he catch me for abandoning his house and rescuing his prisoner? Could it be another group of rebels who think they have caught another lurker and are going to get their thrills from torturing me. The tension kills me. Why is this person just stood there? I can hear their breath slowly on the other side, can smell their blood and the horrible smell of days old sweat penetrating through the gaps in the doorway, making my stomach turn. I can hear a heartbeat so calm and focused. Why do they wait?

The bolt suddenly slides open. My fear rises. The door then is slowly pushed open, scraping the floor as it inches its way. I tense my body and back myself up against the wall. But to my surprise, old man John steps through, looking every bit the war commander he did before, with his black boots and camouflage army gear on. He stands firmly with his hands behind his back. My mouth drops open and I do not say a word, just stare wide-eyed at him.

His face is unreadable as he analyses me. He takes another step towards me, tilts his head to stare me straight in the eyes, then suddenly asks: "How do I smell boy?" He means how does his blood smell, asking if I have any urge to jump him and tear him limb from limb but the thought no longer crosses my mind.

"Horrible," I quickly reply.

Once again, he goes quiet, considering, then suddenly he grins. I think nothing could be more unexpected. He pulls his arms from round his back revealing a small pistol but quickly places it back into his holster. And then, stranger still, he reaches his hand out for me to shake. A rush of joy lashes through me as I shake his hand.

“I have no idea how you did it boy, but you’re still you, and I'm bloody glad you are. I would have hated to have to take you out.”

“Yeah, I wouldn't have been too keen on it either, sir.”

“Alex told me you were ok. But I couldn't believe it properly until I saw it with my own eyes.”

Suddenly another rush of joy lashes over me as I realise that means Alex had made it back, hopefully not too late for Mes either. With the way I remember her looking, she did not have much more fight left in her to keep her alive. Mr Fisher also springs to mind.

“How is Tommy?” I quickly ask.

He smiles gently. “He's fine, thanks to you. He’s got medical care. He’s resting now.”

I relax a little after that.

“How?” he asks me, eagerness and confusion mixed on his face. “How did you beat it? We’ve never been heard of it before.”

I guess my silence speaks volumes about my own confusion as I struggle to find an answer because, before I can even open my mouth in hope that coherent words come out, he speaks again. “It doesn't matter. What matters is that you’re safe, boy.” He nods his head with a serious look of relief on his face. Then he points to me. “Wait right here. Don't move,” he says with a small amount of urgency and seriousness as he walks out of the room. Then I hear the further door scrape open again and not long after, it closes again. This time, the bolt clicks into place.

The room goes silent. I heave a sigh of relief myself, then slowly walk to the cell door to enter the other room. But suddenly I am stopped in my tracks by a figure in the far right of my eye. I can't turn my head as I completely freeze up. My lips quiver but I squeeze them together. My whole body stands stiff with excitement, fear, lust, love - my emotions fly all over the place and I can't hold any of them down. I know who it was. The moment I saw her, the sweet coconut smell of her hair had reached me. My eyes begin to feel warm but I have to fight back the urge to tear up. I can't let her see me like that; what would leak out of my eyes would not be water and would only terrify her.

I hear a small gentle sob, and then the soft beautiful voice of my beloved Kimmy almost whispers my name, "Stuart," she says.

I bite my teeth together and force my head to slowly swivel round to look to her. As I look up from the floor, I feel my heart stop, my throat lump up, my stomach weaken and fill with butterflies as I see the most beautiful person in the world staring back at me. Her big blue eyes are full of tears. The love of my life is holding her hand to her mouth but I can see the smile, a smile so wide it stretches past her palm. Tears of joy stream down her cheeks. I had not even realised it happening but my mouth has stretched too, dare I say further than Kimmy's.

Suddenly nothing that had happened matters: the fact I am no longer human; a century's old monster is probably hunting me; the small mysterious man in my room; the death of the poor innocent girl in front of my eyes, it all just ceases to matter.

"Stuart," she says again, taking her hand away from her mouth and rushing straight into my arms. I throw my arms around her and her sudden touch warms my entire body. Her head pushes against my chest as she sobs louder than ever and squeezing me as if she is never going to let me go again. I have to be cautious though. I do not want to hold her too tight as my strength is now a hundred times what it was before. This does not stop me from squeezing her to the point of cutting off her breath. I lay my head on top of hers and breathe in coconut smell from her golden hair again, almost laughing out loud with happiness from being with her again, to have her in my arms. She grabs my head and stares me in the eyes. Then she throws her lips onto mine, her wet luscious lips smother my own passionately been cautious I don't cut her with my new fangs. Between kisses, she gently says, "I missed you so much," not giving me the time to say it back. "Now don't ever leave me again."

"Never again," I quickly reply pressing my lips onto hers again. "I love you so much, Kimmy."

After several minutes of showing our affection for one another and how much we missed each other, we eventually stop and speak about what had happened to each of us in our separation. All the while, I can't help but think how lucky I am for her to still want me, how I am the luckiest man in the world to be sat with her right now. I can't believe it.

I tell her about Nathaniel and what he did and how he wanted me to join him by killing her father. She makes me laugh by saying, "If I ever see this man, he's going to get a serious piece of my mind."

The image of her giving Nathaniel an old school mother scolding just tickles me too much. "You are amazing, babe." I say back to her. "Everything we have been through and you make me laugh so easily! I love you."

She smiles back at me. "I love you too."

“So what have I missed with you? Where even are we?”

She stiffens up and takes my hand to pull me away from the wall which we both are up against. “Why don't you come see?” she says with a cheeky little grin.

I stand too and keep hold of her hand, not wanting to ever let it go again as we make way for the door. I take the huge metal door and yank it open, once again scraping the floor. We make our way through a small hallway. Marble tiles cover the walls but there is nothing else except another metal door at the bottom, like we are in an underground bunker of some sort.

We reach this door, push it open and in the next room, sitting with John is Alex. He quickly spins around to see us as we walk through. Mes jumps up off her seat, scanning my appearance. I could tell she has noticed how much I have changed. I wonder if Kimmy notices too and chooses not to let it bother her, or had she just overlooked it with the joy of seeing me alive. It must have been harder for her not knowing where I was or if I was even alive. I had the privilege of knowing she had escaped the lurkers who had attacked the camp, which had comforted somewhat, knowing she was likely to be safe with John but she had nothing. No one had known where I was.

“You bloody lunatic!” Alex says as he rushes forward to shake my hand. “I can't believe you made it! Last thing I saw was you ready to take on a bunch of lurkers by yaself. How the bloody hell did you survive that? I couldn't believe it when John said they was bringing you in. Not until I saw it for myself.”

I let out a small chuckle. “It’s good to see you too, mate.”

He slaps me on the back and puts me in a headlock as if we are brothers in a play fight. I guess saving him and his sister has made his feeling towards me much stronger than before.

“Leave the lad alone, Alex.” Mes’ voice comes from behind him as she walks up to me too. Her voice is not as strong as it was and her confidence seems shaken. “I heard what you did for me and my brother. Thank you, Stuart.”

I can see the pain in her eyes. The last time she was awake and saw me, she had me tied up to a chair and was torturing me with a bowl of blood. Not that I blame them, I would had done the same. And who knows, if they hadn’t done that, I might have never had the chance to overcome the lust and fight the urge to become the monster within me.

She goes to open her mouth and her lips quiver as she looks down to the floor. I know what she is about to say so I stop, “Don't worry about it, Mes. You did the right thing. It helped me, it really did.”

She looks at Alex, then to me and gives me a small, quick hug then backs off again without saying anything. She is not into the emotional stuff. It would hurt her image. A quick hug is all I’ll get and I’ll take it. I know she means it.

“Right!” Alex shouts out slapping his hands together, “now that the soppy shite is out of the way, why don't you fill us all in on what happened. I’m dying to know how you escaped them lurkers mate.”

“He didn't,” Kimmy softly says as I work out how best to tell them what I now know. Alex’s face drops.

“What you mean? What happened?”

“I’ll fill you in the details later,” I reply. “I think there is something bigger going on here, bigger than just a rebel war.”

Looks of confusion flash around the whole room as they wait for me to carry on.

I explain what I know, little as it is: the fact that Nathaniel has something in store for the humans, that he spoke of his army, that there might be another group of lurkers fighting against Nathaniel and his people. They don't seem convinced by my lack of knowledge but I try to express that I only know what they allowed me to know. Maybe if I had stayed longer, I could have found out more but I feared for the life of Mr Fisher, he was in such a bad way and another day might have been too long for him.

I can tell John is taking it all into consideration but he is struggling. To him lurkers are still just beasts with one thing on their minds, easy to trick and not capable of forming wider plans. Even my own self isn't enough to convince them. They think I am a miracle case, the one exception. They are being stupid not to listen but I have nothing more to offer than my word.

John comes to a decision and says that we probably have nothing to worry about. I worry but can't think of how best to convince them. But then I have met Nathaniel and they have not. I know he is smarter than any one of us and that there is definitely something coming, but I don't know how to put it into words. I take comfort in the face that, for now, he has no idea where we are and there is no reason for him to be able to find us. I might as well enjoy the relief and use this time to get as much time as I can with Kimmy before something worse happens.

We leave Mes and Alex arguing over which gun they believe is more reliable on the field against lurkers. John had already left taking a bunch of men out for a supply run. The sun is up so I have to stick to the back ends of the camp, away from windows or anywhere a ray of sunshine may enter. Kimmy takes me down a few halls, showing me rooms where the civilians would rest. All this seems to be down in the bunker. She explains that upstairs in the top end becomes a fort at night. From the outside, none of this appears like anything but abandoned buildings, and even if anyone or anything were to find out they were there, reinforced steel shutters automatically cover all the windows and doors at night, strong enough to take the rampage of dozens of lurkers for many nights. The building has generators running the whole building with electricity.

To my ears, this sounds like a five-star hotel for the new world we live in, for the humans anyway. But this is nothing compared to how the higher lurkers are living, lurkers such as Nathaniel. It makes me sick to see good people run down into this, whilst monsters like Nathaniel and that evil witch Claire feast on innocent people every day. But I try to put them and my anger out of my mind. Now is not the time for that kind of thinking, not when I have this beautiful woman glowing with happiness because of how good she believes they have it here.

She takes me to her room, our room as it would be now. As I walk in, I am hit with a wave of shock. The room is good, better than good; it is homely with nice cream and brown wall paper around a king-size bed with brown sheet covers, a cream carpet with a mirror and, of course, it has makeup scattered all over on the top of a dresser. She had told me she had been doing supply runs, looting stores an houses through out the day with a team, a real bad ass rebel now in the few days she had been here, she did it to take her mind off me and make her self useful to the rebels, but she clearly couldn't resist picking up a few makeup supplies during, made me chuckle picturing her raging through abandoned houses looking for foundation.

"This is amazing, Kimmy! It looks..."

"Homely?" she replies with a smile that lights up my very soul. "I didn't want to make it too girly," she says then looks at me with a straight face. A small tear drops but she quickly wipes it away. "I knew you were coming back, Stuart, I knew you weren't gone. Alex would look at me like I was a fool when

I would say it, but I knew. I wasn't ready to say goodbye."

She runs her arm up my chest, around my neck to behind my head then stares me straight in the eyes. "I will never be ready to say goodbye, no matter what."

I place my hand on her cheek and rest my head on hers and take in the warmth of her body as I pull her closer to me with my other arm.

"You have no idea how much I missed this, Kimmy. Your touch, your voice, your beautiful smile, everything about you. But how can you still love me? Look at me. I am ice cold to touch, pale white, a monster."

I walk away filled with shame and place my hands on the doors of the cupboard and stare at myself in the mirror, seeing what Kimmy and everybody else sees when they look at me. I have to drop my head.

I feel a hand slide up my back and grip my left shoulder. She tugs on it gently and turns me around to face her. Then she pulls my head up, by gently lifting my chin. I raise my eyes to see her big blue eyes staring right at me. She has a small smile on her face, not of pity nor laughter, but of comfort.

"You will never be a monster to me, Stuart. I look at you and still see and feel the same person, and I always will. You are the love of my life. That's never going to change."

She leans in and gives me a long and hypnotic kiss that suddenly takes away all my doubt. She breaks away from my lips, which I protest, I would be happy to stay like this all day, just holding each other. But she looks down. "You smell, Stuart. We really need to get you some new clothes." Embarrassment washes over me, with everything going on I never questioned the state of my clothing or the smell that maybe lingers from me.

I let her drag me to a door at the side of the bed but I can't help but laugh.

"What are you doing?" I ask.

"I left the best part out, babe." She swings open the door. "You, mister, are finally going to take a nice hot bath and get out of those scraggy clothes you're wearing."

I look around the door and see a small room with a nice clean bath in it. I can't believe it, I haven't had a real wash in ages. It looks like a god send. She runs in and sits on the side of the tub, gives me a seductive look while pushing out her breasts. "So how do you want it, with or without me?" she jokes and winks then she cheekily sticks her tongue out at me.

"You cheeky monkey," I say winking back, before lifting her off her feet and kissing her on the lips. She squeals with joy as I spin her around. She has her hands on my shoulders and I am looking up at her as we slow. I gently lower her and remove the hair that covers her face then I give her the longest most gentle kiss. The kiss that I have been longing to give her ever since I heard her praying at the old camp. Then I pull away. She looks at me and my face must be straight as hers goes serious. "Is everything ok, Stuart?"

It is, everything is ok, so I give her a little smirk. "Everything is perfect, Kimmy." I look in her eyes. "Just perfect."

We stand for a while just holding each other but eventually we muster the strength to let go. While she goes to get a change of clothes for me, I run the taps, pour in the bubble bath which lies on the side and watch the bath fill up. The moment is so peaceful, just the sound of the water splashing as it fills, bubbling up more and more. I wave my hands through the water when it is done, taking in the warmth then tear my old clothes off and and ease in. The heat fills my whole body and I lie there for what feels like hours, taking in the aroma of the bubble bath.

Then I wake to find Kimmy nudging me and putting most of her strength into the motion and into her words: "Stuart! Wake up. Wake up, Stuart!" She is almost screaming. I spring up, water splashing everywhere.

"What's up, Kimmy? What's the matter?"

"I have been trying to wake you for almost twenty minutes, Stuart! I thought you were dead. You weren't breathing."

She has a seriously scared look on her face but I start to chuckle regardless. "It's not funny Stuart. What the hell?"

"I am sorry, babe. I become weaker through the day now and need sleep. I should have told you before. And I don't breathe really any more. I only need to breath when I am speaking to fill my lungs."

She stands up and throws the towel onto my head. "Yes, you should have told me," she says walking out of the room.

"Are you angry with me?" I shout to her.

"Not decided yet," she quickly replies.

Once I have gotten out of the bath and dried myself, I go back to the bedroom where Kimmy is lying on the bed wearing a cotton white jumper and grey jogging bottoms. She looks inviting and divine. She has jeans and a dark blue shirt out ready for me.

"I've already rolled the sleeves for you."

I laugh, "So I take it you're not that angry with me, then."

She scrunches her face. "Maybe." She stands up and puts her arms around my neck and gives me a quick peck on the lips before smiling. "I thought you might want to check the place out. It's starting to get dim out there," she says as she looks at my wet bare chest. I can see the admiration in her face, and feel the sexual chemistry so, without a second thought, I tip her chin up with my fingers and press my lips onto hers, colliding with each other and I pushed her onto the bed in the same motion. I ease her clothes off and she rips the towel from around my waist and we entwine our bodies together. After showing our love, our affection for one another, for several hours in our new bed, we finally decide to get up for Kimmy to show me around the new camp.

I chuck the clothes on and we set off. We walk up the flight of stairs which leads all the way to the top. When we turn the corner, a group of people sitting together on a sofa and collection of surrounding chairs suddenly stop talking and spin their heads to look at me. The adults grab their children and hold them close. They are afraid of me. They have every reason to be. They have all probably lost loved ones to the lurkers. I can't change that I look like a lurker now, that I am a lurker now.

The room is long. It has sofas all down its length, interspersed with little tables and pool tables and old pinball machines. It reminds me of a social community centre. Kimmy grips my hand, able to tell that I am nervous because of all the fearful and prowling eyes. They make me tense and more like a monster than ever, with the fear and disgust I can see and, more than that, smell coming off them.

As we walk down the room, past the staring group, I give them a small nod. "Hello," I tell myself to say. They reply with low hellos and murmurs, struck by confusion. Nobody here has seen a lurker who did not want to hurt them before. We carry on walking and I can hear Alex's loud voice down at another group of sofas amongst a group of people, some of whom I recognise vaguely from Rotherham camp. One of the men looks at me which draws Alex's attention. He spins around and jumps up, “Stuart! Come here mate. I want you meet everybody.”

As Kimmy and I near, I can hear their heartbeats rise and see their bodies stiffen. None of them take their eyes off me. Hands slowly slip towards their weapons. Alex notices too. “Fucking hell, guys, lighten up. He’s one of us.”

A short guy, black-haired, replies, keeping his expression as it is and his hand on his holster. “He doesn't look like one of us.”

I look at Kimmy and she is hugging my arm while looking up at me. “I am fine, babe. I don't expect people to trust me yet,” I say trying to put her at ease.

“No, this isn't alright, Stuart,” Alex says. “This lad has done what nobody else here has done ever. He’s saved my sister’s life twice and saved my own too by risking himself against a group of lurkers. He’s done more than enough for me to trust him. John trusts him. Mes trusts him, and you will all make my friend feel welcome or, god forgive me, I will kill you all myself.”

They lowered their eyes and, reluctantly, pulled their hands away from their weapons. They slowly come to terms with me being there, accepting what Alex says, that I am different and not going to hurt them. They make space for Kimmy and I to sit down and they begin to ask questions, all the questions they never thought they would be able to ask a lurker without it trying to kill them.

A young nervous lad, small guy, is the first to ask. I had noticed him sit quietly for minutes, scanning my every move. “What's it like?”

I can tell everyone is eager to hear my confession. They all go quiet, even the neighbouring groups go quiet and swivel their eyes and ears in my direction. Kimmy grasps my hand gently to let me know she is there with me.

“You don't need to talk about it if you don't want to Stuart,” Alex says.

"It's fine," I reply. "They want to know." The people start to gather around me like children waiting for a story. I take in a huge breath wondering how to explain and I decide to start from the beginning. "It's difficult to explain. When the change happened, as Alex and Mes know, I wasn't even aware myself. It was a difficult position, I had to be locked up. All I was concentrated on was this smell I could smell. It was so beautiful, so hypnotic, later I knew it was the blood. I knew I had changed when I was alone in that cell in Rotherham camp but I couldn't help myself For a short time, I was a different person and all I wanted to do, all I had on my mind was that smell and what it would be like to taste the blood. It was so overwhelming. Anger was the only emotion running through me and at that point, if I hadn't been tied up, who knows what I would have been capable of, but I beat it."

"How?" the nervous lad quietly asks.

I give Kimmy a long look of admiration. I haven't yet mentioned this to her. "Her," I say nodding at her and then I speak directly to her, "I heard you babe."

She looks at me, confused. "What do you mean?"

"Back in that room, I could hear you praying for me. The pain of hearing it, the suffering I was putting you through, well it brought me back to myself. It gave me the strength to fight through the monster and use you as an anchor to hold onto and break free. I never want to hurt you like that again."

Small beads of tears roll down her cheek and she gives me a gentle kiss on the lips.

"And now? What's it like now?" one of the older men asks.

"In some ways, it's amazing, the strength to do what I can do, being able to hear things and smell things from an unbelievable distance away, never losing breath, it's great. But when I look in the mirror, I see what you see, the paleness, the teeth, and the fact I will live forever and never age frightens me to my very soul, if I even still have one."

It goes quiet again then but the noise level picks up after a while as people start discussing my change. Some of the men believe they could fight against it and become a super rebel like me. The children are shy at first but eventually they want to play with me, like a new toy which has wandered into their camp. Everybody wants to be next to me. They are not nervous of me anymore but have so quickly accepted me. This gives me an overwhelming sense of joy - it's the opposite to what I expected, and to what Nathaniel led me to believe would happen, back in his mansion.

As always, my joy is punctuated by the sounds of war. This time it is a round of shots fired. The men jump for their weapons and look around. The atmosphere of ease and relaxation has been shattered in an instant. I listen hard. I can hear a man screaming, "Do not move. Stay where you are now."

The noise comes from above. "Upstairs," I say.

"What?" Alex replies.

"It's coming from above us."

Alex shouts to the men, "The roof, quick."

They shoot off down the room and we follow. We near a door. Then I hear again, "Don't you fucking move. Stop," followed by another gunshot. I let go of Kimmy's hand and rush past the men, flying up the stairs and close in on the three men, guns pointing out of a gap through a wall which the men are hidden behind. Before they can notice me approach, I am there, beside them staring out through the gap, half expecting Nathaniel to be there. Fear of him has taken over me. I feel the man next to me jump in shock because of my sudden appearance but I ignore him. My eyes are fixed on the figure. Standing there is the mystery man who has appeared in my bedroom. His hands are held up in the air in surrender, his eyes are locked onto mine. Kimmy, Alex and the others catch me up.

"What's going on?" Alex demands.

"There is a man out there, sir. He might be a lurker, I can't tell," the man to my side replies.

"Stuart, we need to talk," the mystery man says. Only I can hear him from the distance we are apart.

"Who are you?" I ask. Kimmy looks at me. "What? Who is that Stuart?"

"It's the man from the mansion who tried to warn me," I reply.

"You aren't safe here, Stuart. None of you are," the man says to me.

Alex closes in to try and see the man more clearly. "What's he saying, Stuart?"

"He says we aren't safe here."

"Do you trust him?"

"I don't know. I need to go out Alex. Speak with him properly."

Kimmy grabs my arm and tugs on it, "No, Stuart, why do you need to go out?"

"He knows something, Kimmy, more than we do and if he's telling the truth about it not being safe, I need to know about it."

John suddenly comes running through, accompanied by Mes and a few others I recognize. "What the hell is going on up here?" he asks loudly and gruffly.

“There's a lurker out there, sir,” Alex replies.

“What? Then kill it.”

I step in. “He wants to talk to me, John. He is warning us, saying we are not safe here. I kind of know him from the mansion. He is the one that warned me then.”

“He's lying. Course we’re safe here. There's no way any lurkers could get in here. Kill him and be done with it.”

One of the men aim to fire. I quickly grab his gun, my speed astonishing them all. “John let me talk to him. What if he's not lying?”

Someone else runs forward and starts an argument, accusing me of being on the lurkers’ side, trying to cause conflict. but Alex soon puts him in his place.

I try again. “John, please, I think he wants to help. There is no way he can get in here by himself. Let me go out and then if it doesn't feel right, do what needs to be done.”

Everybody stares at John awaiting his decision. It’s obvious that even in this new camp, where they have joined the original inhabitants, John is the one everyone looks up to. “Fine. Stuart, find out what he wants and knows and then get away. He could have others waiting in the trees. We can only cover you so much from up here.”

As I go, Kimmy pulls on my arm again. “No, Stuart.”

“It’s going to be fine, Kimmy. He doesn't want to hurt me.”

“How can you be so sure? I'm not losing you again. I only just got you back.”

“I'm not going anywhere babe. I'll be right back, trust me. I need to talk to him."

She finally lets go of my arm. We give each other a long stare before John takes me downstairs and to a small door. He pushes a button dangling from the side on a remote control and the shutter starts to open. He stops it halfway and I duck under and walk out into the middle of the street where the mysterious lurker stands.

Chapter 14

"How did you find us?"

He steps closer, putting me on edge. He sees me tense and immediately stops.

"You don't have to fear me, Stuart. I would never hurt you."

"Why not? You don't even know me."

He looks at me and raises a little smile.

"I have known you your whole life, Stuart. I have been keeping you safe from a distance, making sure you don't get sucked up into my world. But when the bombs dropped, I am ashamed to say, I lost you. I couldn't catch your scent anywhere, that's how I found you here, your scent. After a few months of searching, I gave up, believing you were dead. It killed me. I thought I had failed you, lost you. But even when you were so close to me, I still failed to save you again. I am not going to let that happen again."

I can see the anger and guilt flow through him like a river as he utters the words in disappointment, but all this does is confuse me more.

"But who are you?"

"My name is Richard. Stuart, I am your father."

This word almost knocks me off my feet. Father? This can't be true. This man can't be my real father. This is a ploy, a game of some sort. Maybe he is on Nathaniel's side after all and has been sent to lure me in. I make some mumble of disbelief. He takes another step closer.

"It's true," he insists.

"You're lying. My parents were human. They were just young fools who couldn't handle a child, so they threw me away. You can't be my father."

"Your mother was human, true, but she was no fool. She loved you and would never have given you up."

My frustration flares at the word love.

"Loved me? Really? Then where the hell was she, where the hell were you? You say you've known me my whole life, well then. You watched me grow up. Then you know the shite pathetic life I have had to go through, never having a home, never having a family. If you loved me, if she loved me, then where the hell were you both? I was miserable growing up and you could have changed that?" I still don't quite believe him but it does me some good to get all these frustrations out now that I finally have someone to direct them at.

He drops his head in what I assume is shame but when he raises it again, I see blood leaking from his eyes. They only leave small trails down his cheeks but the shock stops me from continuing to scream at him in anger.

"I saw your life, but I could not, would not bring you into this world of monsters. You might have had a miserable normal life growing up, Stuart, but you were safe, and I didn't want to take that away from you."

"And what about her? What about my mother? If she's human, what's her excuse to leave me to crawl through this world alone."

"She's dead, Stuart." he says with croak in his voice.

I feel a sudden sense of regret and sadness for this woman I have never met or known. Clearly, I do believe him although I'm not sure I want to. I calm myself down. We stand awkwardly for a few minutes as I regain my composure from the sudden news. I have a father. I have to try and process that. While I do, I should hear him out. So we walk to where we will be out of sight of the rebel camp. He explains what happened to my mother, and I can tell he blames himself for the whole thing. He explains everything from the very beginning.

I find it hard to believe him at first but he makes a very convincing argument, once I can get over the fact that he is six hundred years old or there abouts. And he has been fighting Nathaniel for a long time.

Centuries ago, there was a group of leaders who kept the balance between creatures and humans. They didn't kill conspicuously, and the humans knew nothing of their existence. He was a valued member of this group, during the 1500's, and he stood by the leaders, respected their ways and their feelings towards the humans which were always based on the principle of respect. But Nathaniel and his family did not like how things were run. They saw humans as nothing but food, and it turned out a lot of others felt the same way. They could not understand why they should live in the darkness, hidden from the humans, when they could so easily take over and use them. There was a mutiny.

Nathaniel's father led the battle against the Order, as they were called. After a long gruelling battle, the Order lost. Nathaniel and his family became the new Order and things changed dramatically, fast. Lurkers could finally run around and do as they wish as long as they were loyal to the Order. They killed innocents as if it was a game. It was utter chaos.

My father and many others felt for the humans. They always have because there are two kinds of lurker: ones who change and lose all their emotions, become dull to pain, love, regret, and then there are ones like us. We keep our humanity making it easier to fight the blood lust and live from other sources of blood. This makes us stronger because we still have fear so can allow it to take over which gives us that extra strength from the adrenaline which flows through our bodies in battle.

My father and the old guard gathered as many people as they could to them and began their assault on the new Order, not long after they gained power. But Nathaniel's side had the numbers and the money. They were no match and their side was crippled. So, Richard and the old order had to retreat and bide their time as they built a better army, all the while watching this world become darker as the years drew on.

Then with the 1800's, technology grew which finally gave them a fighting chance. They were winning the war, taking back the Order, more and more lurkers started to embrace my father's side. A woman named Sarah rose up through the ranks and helped the rebellion. He sounded quite fond of her as he explained she was their leader now. He said there was no more loyal person to him than she. Sarah ran the family out of power for more than a century, managing to keep the war hidden away to the past and had peace for over a century at least.

Then my father found my mother, Rebecca. Such a beautiful name. It was a pleasure to listen to him describe her. She sounded amazing: strong but gentle, cared for everything, saw the best in everyone. Even when he first explained what he was, she did not judge him or see him as anything else but the man she saw and knew. He was taken by her instantly. The more he describes her, the more I can't help but think about Kimmy; he was describing my mother and my girlfriend as one person. I tell him about Kimmy and he replies, "Blessed to have such a person."

The best ten years of his life, he claimed, out of all the centuries he had lived. There had been nobody like Rebecca to him. He tried to leave it all behind when I was born and left Sarah in charge. Then one day, Nathaniel's men came for him, knowing he was no longer protected by the rebels. My mother was in the house alone. My father had taken me out on a walk and, on the way back to the house, he heard screaming shouting. He ran back to the house to help, but it was too late. the attackers were already gone. In the next room, my mother lay dying. He ran to her aid but she was bleeding out too fast, so he went to bite her, to change her, but before he could, she died. I felt his pain. If I was to lose Kimmy, my whole world would seem no longer worthwhile.

"When a person's greatest love is taken from them, nothing else much matters, and he becomes lost in his own grief," he says. I can believe it. I can't remember anything of my mother, but she did not deserve to die that way. My anger towards Nathaniel intensifies and the urge to tear his head off rages in me as it did in my father. But he had me, the only thing left of her, and he knew she would have wanted him to get up and carry on living without revenge in his heart. She had been such a kind warm person, if only I could remember her. He wasn't going to let me have the same fate, and he knew Nathaniel would be back to destroy him and everything he loved. So he gave me up and told no one about me. Things changed for my father then. The war didn't matter, Nathaniel didn't matter, keeping me safe was the only option. He left everything behind and watched me grow up from afar, that is until the bombs dropped and, as he said, he lost me.

"What happens now?"

He takes a minute to pull himself away from reliving the regret and loss of my mother. He visibly focuses on me and my question and responds.

"Your people are not safe. Nathaniel is coming to round them up and use them like cattle."

I'm not following. "Cattle?"

"That is their plan, the culmination of all their years of planning. They are farming the humans, rounding them up into the camps to create a never-ending supply of food, and they plan to begin with your rebels."

This horrible news, while producing a visceral reaction in my stomach, does not actually shock me. Nathaniel is pure evil and it makes sense. It seems right down his alley to pull something like this off, creating human farms around the world, locking them up, breeding them, feeding them. The cycle would perpetuate until every human in the world had become a dumb animal that would not know any better than the farms they were born into. The idea is horrific. We have to do something.

"But how can he know where we are?"

"Your scent, Stuart. If they have a tracker follow your steps, eventually it will lead them right here."

At that moment, I know what I have to do, but it means doing the one thing I had just promised Kimmy I would never do again, leave her. But if I don't and they are able to keep up with my scent, it won't matter if we move from this camp, they will only track me to the next camp. It is going to be a hard decision to submit to but my mind is already made up. I have got to keep her and everybody else safe and stop them from becoming part of this disgusting operation. It has to be done.

"You know what has to be done Stuart," my father says regrettably. He is right. I do. "You will be able to return but only after the threat is gone. We have safe places for you to hold out in. We have taken the mansion. We won't let this happen to anybody. Nathaniel will finally meet his end when we find out where he plans on starting this. But until then, you must leave, to keep them safe, to keep her safe."

My mind doesn't register up everything he is saying. I am set on one thing: the thought of Kimmy's reaction when I tell her. The very thought of it is enough to make my eyes well up. But I do hear him say I am to hide out in a safe place whilst this plays out and that sounds absurd. It is not something I am willing to do. It does not matter what he says, I will not run and hide from this. I don't say this yet though. I have something more important to do first.

"You have to let me say goodbye."

He gives me a gentle nod.

"Do not take too long. They could already be on their way here."

We both walk together back to the series of buildings which act as the base so that I can say my goodbyes but suddenly my father grabs me by the arm. "Wait," he whispers.

"What is it?"

He sniffs, flaring his nostrils and turning his head to each angle trying to pinpoint the smell. He finally nods his head towards the woods, but I see nothing.

“Somebody's here.”

The street is quiet; the wind gently blows the dry leaves from the autumn drop. They scrape across the floor. Then, as I concentrate, I can smell what my father can. An odd mix fills my nostrils, the smell of perfume covering the strong smell of dry blood. Then we hear the sound of heels clicking on the tarmac of the road, the sound echoing louder and louder until Claire steps out from around the corner. She is instantly recognisable even out of her usual evening dress. Somehow, she even makes regular clothes look effortless regal and seductive. Her shirt is unbuttoned just to the point of immodesty and her jeans hug her legs in a way which suggests indecency. she looks at both of us together then smiles that dreadful evil smile I’ve come to know.

“Sorry. Did I interrupt the father-son reunion? How touching. How terrible of me. I am dreadfully sorry.”

The very sight of her fills me with anger and hatred. The desire to rip her head off is strong. I step forward ready for the attack but my father grabs me by the shoulder to stop me.

“She's not alone, Stuart.”

I look behind her, into the dark woods. He’s right. I see gleaming eyes amongst the shadows. Then out step dozens of lurkers who form an arc behind Claire.

I can hear John in the distance, possibly the rooftop, screaming to his fighters to get to their posts but I know an attack of this magnitude would be too much for them to handle. The fort will keep them safe. It would take a full army to get through those walls. There are about twenty or so lurkers in total. No matter how strong they are, they don't have the numbers to break through.

"My, my, they really have out done themselves this time. The humans are really becoming smarter," Claire says patronizingly.

"You can't get through Claire, you know that?" my father says in a proud certain, matter of fact way. I can tell he is a strong-willed person and that he is not at all afraid of this gang of lurkers in front of him.

"Maybe, maybe not, but we won't know until we try, will we now Richard? But I think we might need to rid ourselves of you two first. I won't pretend that I won't enjoy it."

"Stuart, go," my father says to me.

"What?"

"Go. I'll hold them off long enough for you to escape. Your friends will be safe for now."

The idea of leaving him now is ridiculous so I ignore his command, shift position and get into a fighting stance. I stare straight at Claire, letting him know that I am ready to fight by his side. He grasps me by the shoulder causing my to spin my head towards him in shock, and he gives me a long hard look, I guess that this is his way of letting me know he's proud of me.

"I am sorry son," he says gently whilst turning back and keeping his face firmly forward. The word "son" washes over me and comforts me. It feels so nice to finally have a true dad, one that would risk his life for me. I only wish I had known him longer. Seeing him now, I know this is a man I could have very much looked up too and be proud to call a father.

From the way Claire looks at both of us as she prepares her attack, I understand what my father meant when he said she had no emotions except maybe anger and hatred, no other feelings towards anyone but herself. Her straight look says it all. She is not bothered by what might happen to anybody here but herself. The lurkers surrounding her are just a distraction so she can get a hold of my father. She clearly does have some anguish towards him, I can see that. It's probably something that happened a long time ago, before I was even born. Whatever it was, it had turned into something cold and calculated and I am sure she is about to get her revenge.

"Pathetic," she snorts. Then she opens her arms and every one of the lurkers simultaneously starts to sprint towards us. There are too many of them. My fear grows with every step they take towards us. Everything seems to be in slow motion. I tense my body and let the warmth of anger and fear take over me. Two dozen lurkers are raging towards us, not slowing down, only gaining speed. They are so close that I can see the gleam of moonlight glinting off their fangs. I look to my father one last time. He looks back, nods, then sets off running towards the lurkers. Seeing him without fear flying towards them gives me the strength to push my legs into gear and follow, stride after stride, gaining speed. I can feel my strength growing, my body pumping ready for action. Then suddenly gun shots fly over our heads, taking lurker after lurker down to the floor. It's the snipers from the roof shooting from behind us. Seeing the lurkers drop, knowing we aren't fighting alone, sends a jolt of hope through me and with that I take one huge leap towards the first lurker, striking him in the chest. We both fall to the ground. I quickly fling my arm around in a backhand swing to strike the next lurker throwing himself my way, and I connect with his jawline. I hear the crack as my arm slams across his face and his yell of pain as he skids across the hard concrete, ending up metres from where he started and scraping the skin of his back as he does so.

I look and try find my father but before I can catch a sight of him, another one grabs me and throws me across the road slamming me up against the kerb. Pain shoots through my body like a dart. I feel one of my ribs crack on the kerb, but without hesitation I jump back up to find two lurkers in front of me. One of them grabs my head whilst the other cripples my legs taking me to my knees. Suddenly another shot takes the one that has my head down, releasing me and shocking the other lurker enough to give me time to swipe their feet away then snap a neck. The body thumps to the floor beside me. I jump back to my feet, ignoring the shooting pain from my ribs, trying to scan the battlefield for my father but he is surrounded by too many lurkers. I run and throw myself on three of them taking them to the ground.

As I return to my feet, I find my father has Claire on the floor and he is tugging at her head. Her scream is so loud and at such a pitch it hurts my very ears, a noise so disturbing it could smash glass. Before he could detach her head from her body, three more lurkers jump on him taking him down to his knees and he struggles to keep his hold on her. I go to his rescue but, like him, I am suddenly surrounded and thrown to the floor directly in front of him. We try to break free but there are just too many holding us down. Even a lurker as old as my father cannot possibly take on that many by himself. Unable to move, we both just stare at one another, knowing what is just moments away from us. Going like this is not how I imagined it would be, but this time, I get to go out fighting with my father who I have had the privilege to meet before I was gone from this world.

Everything seems to be moving so slowly. I watch Claire get to her feet and making her way towards my father. I see him staring me in the eyes as blood leaks down his face from both eyes. In the distance, I can hear Kimmy screaming, crying out my name. I look up to the roof and see rebels trying to pull her back from the edge but not succeeding as she clings on to the gap in the wall with everything she has, tears streaming from her face. Suddenly tears of blood splash out from mine too from the sight of her in pain. My fight has gone out of me. My life flashes before my eyes as I feel the sudden tug on my head as something tears at my neck. All the moments I had with Kimmy scroll through my mind: back in university when we first met, when I was a bumbling idiot, the quiet and peaceful time we spent in the cottage together, all the love we shared together, the laughter, the sad moments. Nothing passes through my mind but Kimmy - the only good thing that came to me in this life. She saved me from all the loneliness from never having a family growing up. She gave me that family. Kimmy was my family and I was happy. Suddenly I feel at peace and close my eyes ready for the end to come.

Then to shatter that peace, the alarms siren as the huge reinforced shutters begin to lift open. They are the only thing keeping the lurkers away from the humans, the only things keeping Kimmy safe. I scream out loud, screaming with everything I have telling them to close the doors, but suddenly wave after wave of rebels pour out, shooting consistently.

"NO! What are you doing? Close the doors! Get back inside! Close the fucking door!" I scream as one by one the lurkers leave us on the ground and shoot off to attack the rebels pounding towards them. I watch some of them get taken down and others charge through as if they are passing through water. Suddenly I feel my body rise from the floor - I am still screaming for them to stop - and fly through the air. My head suddenly cracks against a solid wall.

Chapter 15

My eyes suddenly spring open. I find myself face down in a puddle of blood. I splutter. The pain from my head quickly dissipates as the wound heals itself. I expect screams of pain and the sounds of fighting but instead I hear nothing. Everything is totally quiet. I slowly bring myself to sit up and scan the area. Fear and sadness run through my body like a gust of wind as I see dozens of bodies laid out, scattered over the street, all dead. My father is also a few metres away from me, bringing himself back around to consciousness. I can only assume they did the same to him as to me. I bring myself up to my feet and force myself to face the horror of what lays in front of me. Body after body of young soldiers lie across the street. So many are torn to pieces, most of them are not recognisable. I look across to my father. His face says the same as mine must. Both of us are distraught. We slowly make our way, without speaking through the bodies towards the building. We enter through the huge shutter door and a little way into the first room, I see Alex kneeling down. He looks up at me with nothing but pain and anguish in his face. The red burns around his eyes are a clear sign that he has been crying.

When I reach him and look down, my sadness only grows. With difficulty, I hold back my own tears to see John lying dead on the floor in front of Alex. His throat is torn open. I dare not ask the question but I have to. My mind is running over all the possibilities of what could have happened to her. And of course, that leads to the worst scenario which then takes over my mind. If it is true, I have not the slightest idea what I would do.

“Alex,” I say gently, bringing his head back up to look to me. “Did they…” I’m not even been able to finish the sentence without choking up, bringing my own tears out. “Did they,” I try to say again but fail. “Is she?”

He replies quickly before I utter the word and fully break down, “No.” He shakes his head. “They gathered the women, took them away”.

I kneel down in front of Alex and place my hand on his shoulder. “John was a good man, Alex.”

He rubs his eyes with his sleeve. “He was like a father to me these last months. He went out fighting though. He went out like a soldier.”

“And Tommy?” I ask, hoping they would have left him given the condition he is in.

“They took him too.”

He raises himself to his feet with a resigned but determined sigh. “We need to get them back Stuart, Mes, Kimmy, Tommy, all of them.”

The sudden mention of Kimmy's name silences me and sends me into a whirlwind thinking about where she is, how scared she must be.

“We will,” my father says for me. “My friends are out looking for where they will be taken as we speak. They might have already found it.”

Alex reaction to my father was quick, as he pulled a gun an pointed it at him.

“we were all fine till you showed up, who the fuck are ya”? he shouts

My father does not react just stares remorsefully, “did you fucking bring them here, answer me” he screams.

I reach out slowly and push Alex’s gun down, he looks to me with tear filled eyes wanting an explanation, I just shake my head, he knew it wasn't his fault, he drops the gun and falls silent.

"Is there anyone else left?" I ask Alex finally to break the dead silence as we all look around in horror.

"I'm not sure, it was a massacre. I stopped looking for survivors when I found him." There's another long pause.

"Why?" I say body shaking from the anger of losing her again.

"Why what?" Alex replies as I clearly don't mean, why did he stop looking.

"Why did you open the shutter! How could you be so stupid, Alex? There were too many of them and now look what's happened! The men are dead Kimmy and Mes are god knows where. Why?"

I try to refrain from shouting but I can see the regret in Alex's face; he knows he made the wrong choice. I immediately feel guilty for losing my temper.

"We couldn't just let you die, Stuart. You're one of us."

It turns out that it is hard to be angry at somebody who was trying to save my life. It's obvious he made the wrong decision. My life was not worth all these other lives. We've lost everyone. I am trying to be strong but to have lost Kimmy again after such a short time back together is tearing me apart. If anything was to happen to her now, I'd be even more responsible and, more than ever, I cannot bear it.

After we round up what is left of the base camp - a couple dozen men, half of whom are injured - Alex groups together a few trucks of those which are left. Those who have the strength fill the trucks with the bodies, my father and I end up doing most of the work, and we drive them to a nearby field. After an hour or so of digging, we bury the bodies and give them all a proper burial. John's is torture for Alex and I.

Alex decides he needs to say a few words, "John found me and Mes two months after all this shit started. We weren't doing so good. He took us in, taught us how to fight, gave us what we needed. He saved us. We were ready to give up, ready to leave this horrid place we still call home, but he said, he said that if we all just laid down and gave up, then they deserve to win. This is our world, our home and those sons of bitches better believe that we are not going down without a fight. He wasn't the greatest with words but that, that meant something to me and he was right. We might be backed up against the fence injured but we are not going to give up, not now, not when our people need us the most, and John, he went out fighting because he believed we can win this, and so do I."

I look around and see the determination and hope growing in the faces around me. They all needed something to believe in and somebody to lead them, and with just a few words, Alex has just indisputably taken that position.

Once we are back at the camp, Alex orders the men to gather all the armoury they can find and fill up the trucks. My father advises us to make our way to the mansion as a place of safety and to see if Sarah had returned with news of where we might be able to find the captives. It will be safer for the men to come along with us as this place is no longer safe - the attackers had killed the generators, shutting off all the electricity meaning that we are unable to close the shutters.

My father and I sit by the door on a sofa, on guard for wandering lurkers. The pain in my face as I think about Kimmy must be visible as he tries to comfort me. "We will find her, Stuart. They're not going to hurt her. They need them all alive and healthy for their plan."

This gives me little comfort but a little is better than none at all. I try to take my mind of Kimmy and her situation so I ask, "Claire. She has it in for you. Why?" He gives me a little smile and leans back into the sofa.

"I believe it was around 1910. Before the human war. We were over in France fighting. We were trying to get Nathaniel's father, Demetrius. Cut of the head of the snake, you know. I was in his chateau, but found myself surrounded by Claire and a few of her minions, and I escaped her, by throwing her dog onto the open fire." He grimaces slightly either to hide or laugh or from remorse, it's unclear.

The story makes me laugh out loud. I had been expecting some dramatic story of how he had slain somebody for whom she cared dearly.

"Are you serious?" I say through the laughter.

"Yes," he insists. "It was my only option, I really wasn't going to make it out of there and then the dog runs past me. I knew she was as fond of it as she could be fond of anything. It distracted her enough for me to flee."

"That poor dog," I say cheerfully.

"Well it was rather me or the dog."

"Oh not because of you, you probably did it a favour."

He looks at me in confusion, "How do you mean?"

"Well it had to bear listening to her every day. Poor thing was probably going insane, for all you know it was already running toward the fire."

He lets a loud chuckle and throws his arm around my shoulder. "Yes, you're probably right there."

“Stuart.”

Alex's voice comes from behind us. We both stand and spin around to see what was up, our faces solemn once more.

“We are ready. How long will it take to reach the mansion? We don't have long until the sun will be up.”

“We will make it before then, Alex,” my father replies.

So everybody piles into the trucks with few words exchanged and we set off on our way. It feels like I am going back on myself, back to the mansion I had to escape from just two nights ago. I am in this truck with Alex, my father and four others. The rest of the survivors are in the other three trucks which follow us. There is an armoury in the back of each of them, ready for war. I am determined to rescue Kimmy no matter what, I will not go through the same pain my father had to endure of losing my mother.

“Are you sure about the mansion father”? I hesitate after calling him father a word I have never called anybody, warmth touched me with the word aswell as nerves as I look at his expression, I don’t want to dwell on it so I carry on. “What if Nathaniel returned and took it back?”

“A great number of our oldest and best were left there, ready for any attack. I will be surprised if he has taken it back so quickly son.” with that word my nerves drop and comfort over flows me. son.

After just more than an hour of flying over the empty motorway, we find ourselves back in Rotherham and have the mansion in our sight. I can see the men becoming more nervous as we near, not knowing what waits ahead. We pull up to the huge metal gates and my father tells us all to wait here whilst he checks it out. He clears the fence in a bound and perches by the door for a few seconds before he enters. Waiting for him, I am on edge. It's unnerving to be back here. I need to move as I am getting so restless waiting. I am about to leave the car when the door suddenly reopens and my father comes walking nonchalantly out with another lurker by his side. She's a small woman with long dark hair, she has a strong presence about her.

I leave the truck as they open the gates and come towards us.

"Sarah, I would like you to meet my son, Stuart." Ah so this is Sarah. She looks quite unassuming rather than what I would expect the leader of the Order to look like. She gives me a long hard firm shake whilst looking at me as if I am a cute puppy.

"Nice to meet you Stuart. No doubt Richard, he is definitely your son. Look at those big puppy dog eyes. I suppose you don't know nothing of me?" she says.

"Actually, I know a little. My father has mentioned you a few times."

"Has he now?" she says with a grin in my father's direction. "Not all bad I hope."

"What's the situation?"

Sarah's face tightens and she gives me a look of pity. My father must have told her about Kimmy and the others already. She looks into the line of trucks, giving the men the same look.

"Is this all who made it?"

"It was a massacre," my father says with regret. He carries so much weight on his shoulders, he clearly feels like it is his duty to protect everybody, and that he has let them down - the same way I feel about Kimmy. "I could not save them."

"It's not your fault." Alex's voice rises up from behind us as he too steps out of the truck. He walks around to the front to stand with us and quickly places his hand on my father's shoulder. "There was nothing you could have done. There were too many of them and it was our decision to open the doors. If anyone is to blame, it's us."

The rest of the men are now out of the trucks and are looking anxious and a little scared. They are out before sunrise surrounded by a small army of lurkers, they have every right to be a little nervous. But they are here and we all want the same result: to get our friends and families back and take down the monster that is Nathaniel for good.

"We tracked down a few strays who made it out of the house," Sarah lets my father know. "We followed them to a building just at the edge of town, a few miles from here. It's heavily guarded. It could be the place."

I quickly jump into gear at the thought of being able to get Kimmy back sooner than expected.

"Great! What are we waiting for?" I say heading back to jump in the truck.

"Stuart, wait," my father quickly replies. "We don't know what waits there. They might not even be there."

"Or they might be there, and we can go get them back right now," I snap back at him, not thinking about anything else. I am consumed by the thought of the fear Kimmy must be in, the things they could be doing to her. I dread to think what will happen if Claire finds out that Kimmy is my girlfriend. What would she do to her for the trouble I have caused and for the years of trouble my father has caused her and Nathaniel - it would be nothing less than pure evil.

"Or it could be a trap." I suddenly hear from Sarah snapping me out of these thoughts and back to reality.

“Trap or not, these are our friends and family. I can't sit here and do nothing.”

I look at Alex expecting his support and for him to follow, but he just stands there, staring at me.

“You aren’t coming?”

He makes a noise but what is intended to be words becomes but a pant of air as it leaves his mouth.

“You're just going to sit here and let them take Mes?” I shout at him in anger. How can he not jump at the opportunity of getting his sister back? I stare at him and the men forcefully and they gradually start to move back towards the trucks with no enthusiasm. There doesn’t seem to be any desire in them to save their loved ones, causing me to ram the truck door open. Just as I go to jump in, my father grabs my arm gently, seeing the frustration I am in. He knows the pain I'm going through all too well.

“Now is not the time to act fast, Stuart. That is how mistakes are made and friends are lost. Take a good look at these men.”

My eyes shoot towards Alex.

“They need rest son.”

I focus and he’s right. Now I can clearly see the heavy bags beneath his eyes, the sweat dripping from his head, how his body hunches over but he forces himself to keep standing, the pain and grief in his eyes, the lines on his face. The rest of the men are the same way. I had been blind with frustration and forgot that I am no longer the same as them; I won't tire, I won’t weaken. But Alex and the men have been up for almost two nights straight, carrying and burying our dead, the friends and family who have already been lost in this war. Their bodies are running off fumes. I can't be selfish. This is not only about

Kimmy and I; this has become so much bigger to all of us.

Sarah walks up and stands beside of my father and gently takes my other arm.

"Let the men rest. We have people keeping an eye on the building. If anything is to happen, we will know straight away, Stuart."

I think about Kimmy, but I also realize that I would be leading them into a slaughter if I were to make them follow me. I can't treat them like pawns for my own benefit. If there is something simple, I can do to prevent them dying unnecessarily, I have to do it. I don't want this war to turn me into a monster like Claire and Nathaniel.

The men settle into the mansion. Most of them are stunned by the old building as they have never lived in anything bigger than a two-bedroom flat or council house, and have never seen the inside of a stately home like this in person. They are all taken aback by the length of the rooms and the comfort of being able to sleep in a real house feeling safe for a change. They have adapted surprisingly well to the idea that they will be guarded by lurkers and we are what will keep them safe as they sleep.

I can't feel safe here though. I see a nightmare each time I close my eyes which being back here reanimates and makes vivid again. It's an image I will never be able to forget; there was nothing but evil in this house when I was only here only a few days ago. The men go straight to sleep when they have explored the house and settled into rooms.

It is a little after midnight now. I haven't slept myself for a while but my body doesn't seem to notice. Alex wanted to stay with me and keep watch but I forced him to go rest and regain his strength as he is going to need it. So now I'm alone. I have perched myself on the roof of the mansion, sitting with my legs hanging off the edge, taking in the fresh air of the night. It may be dark but

I don't miss a thing. I can see every little fly drifting in the sky, every little bug creeping through the night. I can hear the almost silent muffled flap of an owl's wings as it swoops across the sky. It is as if each creature goes into slow motion until another noise sparks my attention and my concentration shifts. It is another amazing dark gift for the price of immortality. I see other lurkers walking around the house, passing the front gate and walking together down the garden, guarding the mansion every little bit like it is a sanctioned military base, which I guess it is now.

Suddenly Sarah appears beside me. My resulting jump of shock almost makes me fall of the roof. I heard nothing. She must have been sneaking up on people for centuries.

"It's beautiful, isn't it? The night, when you just watch, listen," she says ignoring my shock and peering away into the night.

"It is," I reply in kind. It is beautiful when you just let it take over.

After a while of sitting together in pure silence, she says, "She will be ok Stuart. They don't want to kill her, they need her."

I know she is right. They aren't going to hurt her or any of them if we are right about their future plans. It might be true but the pain is still there and it will remain with me until she is back in my arms, safe.

She gives me a little smile. "You know your father and I used to come up here, before Nathaniel and his family took over of course, and we used to just sit here in this spot and talk, sometimes all night. Strange you should pick the same place."

I can tell she had cared for my father. They have known each other a very long time, such a long time I can barely comprehend it. But a part of me thinks that maybe she cared for him just a little more than he knows.

"He hasn't been the same, your father I mean, since she was taken from him. He drifted away from us, from everything. He became a little darker, a little more dead inside."

It's a funny expression to use given his situation but I know what she is getting at. I can see that there is a little pain in her eyes, but she just keeps staring out into the night, and does not look at me once. "You should get some rest Stuart," she finally says turning my way. "The sun will be up shortly."

I smile at her and leave her on the perch spot on the roof, meditating on the night. I climb down and head back into the mansion. On my way back to the room I stayed in last time, I hear a noise coming down the corridor. I follow the echo of what sounded like a battle. There's a strange knocking, irregular sounds. The striking sound gets louder as I reach one door, I slowly turn the handle and pushed the door open entering a big empty room, like an old-fashioned version of a sports hall. There is a painted ring in the middle on the smoothed and shiny floor and my father stands in the middle of the circle holding a wooden stick shaped as a sword, surrounded by wooden sculptures of men holding the same kind of wooden swords. His concentration does not falter as I enter, and with a few quick movements of his arms and a few deft steps the wooden statues are sliced in two and scattered across the room. Even as a lurker myself, it is difficult to keep track of my father's movements. The curtains cover the windows but I can see that the sun is now rising through them.

"Grab a sword, son," I hear him say, but due to how unexpected his words are, I don't reply.

"I know you are not going to listen to me and stay here whilst we fight

Nathaniel. I can see that. So you need to know how to fight."

I rail against his assumption that I cannot protect myself even after he has seen me fight against Claire and her goons the night before. I reply rather sharply.

"I can fight."

He turns towards me with a look showing a hint of his more ferocious side that I have yet to witness. So far, he has always been so calm, even when facing death. It would have to be something truly horrible to bring that animal out of him and I don't think that would be something I would like to see, let alone be on the receiving end of.

"You are strong for a young one, I know that, but going up against Nathaniel and his best men, will be quite a bit more challenging then you may be thinking. So, grab a sword," he says tersely, not changing his strong stance or look.

I walk up to where a few wooden swords are hanging on racks attached to the wall and take one down. It's so light, it feels almost like there is nothing in my hands except a texture.

I slowly walk up to the ring not breaking eye contact with my father, and his eyes are no laughing matter, he is serious. I feel a surge of fear even though I am facing my own father. The intensity of the moment takes me and I grip the sword by the hilt with both hands and I shudder from either fear or nerves. Regardless, I raise the sword up high.

"Spread your legs further apart," he says. "You need a firm stance to be able to balance yourself when attacked."

I widen my stance, glancing at his feet and then my own to match and with a swift movement he has the sword poised less than an inch away from my neck.

"Don't ever take your eyes off your opponent, no matter what."

He pulls his sword back and takes his stance once again.

I stand firmly, waiting for his attack. I can see him examine my stance, then he swings the sword to my head. I raise my own to block and they clash together with a loud crack and whip noise which echoes around the room. The force pushes me backwards and without giving me a chance to re calibrate, he swings and cracks my legs, the force of this hit lifting me into the air and sending me crashing onto the ring on my back. And the sword is suddenly in my face.

"Don't ever lose focus," he says standing back to allow me to gather myself again and get to my feet.

I take my stance once again, ready for what he has to offer. He swings again for my head and I swing back again clashing the swords together. Then he steps to the left with lightning speed, spinning around and swinging the sword to my chest. I narrowly avoid it, think I see an opening for his neck and go for the attack but, before I know it, he parries the attack and strikes me in the chest with his elbow and slings me over his head with such speed that it nearly cracks the ring floor.

Taking in the pain from the blow to the chest, I raise myself back to my feet in anger and grip the sword tighter and swing at him strike after strike, and blocking all those he returns until he does one deft movement, spinning around to my other side. Holding onto my anger, I keep track and swing the sword back over my head trying desperately to hit him, but he grabs the sword, pulls it out of my hands and strikes the back of my legs. This forces me to my knees and he throws the sword around my neck into a choke hold.

"Anger isn't the way for you, Stuart," he says into my ear letting me go and throwing me once again across the ring. "If you let anger take over you in battle, you will become like them Stuart, uncontrollable. You need to fight with another emotion. It's a need not a want. We fight because we need to. If you can't beat Nathaniel, what is going to happen to you? What is going to happen to your friends?" his voice grows louder, "What will happen to Kimmy?"

With this mention of Kimmy's name, I begin to feel warm, my body tightens up and my head begins to boil. Tears almost leave my eyes and it becomes painful, so painful I have to grab my head and drop to my knees, crying out.

"Control it, Stuart," my father shouts. "Use it, use it. Without it, she dies. Without it, we lose." Suddenly my body tightens up, the pain goes away. I think about losing Kimmy, and I rush to my feet and then towards my father, ready to fight. He slashes the sword at my hands, I catch it, blocking with my own sword and swing it at him. He blocks, swings, parries. I block, swing, parry. The dance continues longer this bout. To both our surprise, I parry his next move and jump behind him and, before he can turn, I place the sword against his neck. He lowers his sword and turns around with a proud smile on his face.

"Good, very good son."

I can feel the power surging through me, but unlike all the other times anger had not taken over and I don't have any desire to tear my way through whatever blocks my way this time. I still feel somewhat in control.

We train for a while longer and before we know it the sun is at its highest and my body begins to weaken. My loss of strength is visible. I haven't slept for a while and my father notices and sends me off to my room to sleep through the day. On my way to the room, I see humans taking over guard duty from the lurkers, and the sight of us working together, makes me think there could be a future in this world, without wars and battles between the two species; a truce of some kind, but with Nathaniel and his family ruling the lurkers, this is impossible.

I come across Alex on the way, sitting talking to Sarah by the staircase. She herself looks a little out of energy, and he looks no better than he did in the early hours when we arrived here.

I hear Sarah offer to show him around. They seemed to have clicked which is good; Alex is now the leader of this rebellious group of humans, or what is left of it, and Sarah is by all means the leader of the Lurker rebels. The two of them together with their fighters working as one would be a brilliant team. This gives me hope that we will save our people, and that we will save Kimmy.

Chapter 16

I spring awake as a sack of clothes lands on my head. My father stands there with a smile on his face.

"That would have been way too easy if I was an intruder. Your senses need feeding. Your body's weak. You should have picked me up before I reached the room." He walks towards the door. "Get them on and meet me at the edge of the woods."

He leaves and I get out of bed and open the curtains. I can hear the sound of rain as it splashes heavily on the window. The sound causes a nice chill to run up my spine. The sound has always calmed me, even as a human it was the one thing that would put me to sleep without a doubt. It is night-time - the clock on the stand shows 7pm - I grab the sack and empty it onto the floor, revealing wellington boots, a rain coat and a jogging suit. I chuck them on and leave. On my way through the house to the main doors, I stop as I hear Alex and a few others in the dining room. I decide to pop my head in to see how they are doing. On my way through the door, I can't avoid looking at the end of the table where Nathaniel had killed that poor girl, and the images once again run through my head vividly. This is followed quickly by the thought of what he could do to Kimmy, if he finds out that she is important to me. How he would torture her for my actions against him! Familiar feelings of anger surge through my body, but I can hear my father's voice in my head, shouting as he did in the gym, "use it, USE IT" and it all becomes easier to control.

I hear someone call my name loudly, bringing me away from the nightmare and back to the table where Alex is tucking into his dinner, along with the men left from the camp.

"Everything alright, mate?" he says with a look of confusion on his face.

"I'm fine, just lost in thought."

"I know what ya mean, I can't stop thinking about..."

"Then we need to go get them!" one of the men shouts from down the table, hitting the table with his fist in anger.

"We are not ready to go yet," Alex whimpers out in both disappointment and shame. "Sarah has warned me of their army. There are too many of them and we don't know anything yet about the place they are been held at."

“Since when do we listen to lurkers? My family are held there,” the same man shouts.

“And so is mine. And Stuart’s, and nearly everybody else’s here, but right now it would be a death march,” Alex snaps back.

Suddenly more men jump in with their opinions bringing everyone to their feet in an argument.

Alex observes for a while and then slowly gets to his feet as the men all argue with each other about what we should do, talking over each other. Some want to stay here, and I guess they have no loved ones captured otherwise they could never feel that way. Others bang the table in anger, yelling at each other in debate. Nonetheless they all look to Alex for an answer, and it’s clear he does not have one.

I can see the frustration in his face. He is hurting; hurting because he has lost Mes to the monsters and hurting because he now has to be the unlikely leader since his friend and mentor John had gone.

He looks to me uneasily as the men grow louder and more aggressive. I can tell he is lost but he is in charge, and he needs to show the men that. He could be that leader, I know that, and I am very sure the men know that, but Alex is unsure.

I scowl at Alex pointedly, meaning for him to take control, but he eventually sinks back into his chair and just watches as the men fall apart becoming less an army ready to fight the undead and more a bunch of brawlers at a bar.

And in that moment, I am hit by a wave of shock. What am I seeing? I can see it in Alex's face, but the men are too busy arguing and haven’t noticed yet. I cannot believe it - he has just given up. In that very moment, he let go and dropped back into his chair, giving up.

One by one, they march out of the dining room shouting in anger until only Alex and I are left in the room. He stares into the abyss of his own mind as I walk up to him and take the seat by his side.

"What the hell are you doing Alex?" I snarled.

He eventually looks my way. "What do you expect me to do Stuart?"

"I expect you to take control of your men, get them ready for when we go get everyone back..."

"We can't!" he shouts, stopping me in my tracks. "You didn't see them at the camp Stuart. I did. I saw it all. When the doors opened, they took over us like we were ants, and that was my call. John trusted me with my decision and look where he is now! Look where they all are! We didn't stand a chance then, and we don't now."

I grab him by the shoulders in anger. "Yes, we do stand a chance, you idiot. My father and Sarah have an army. You have an army, even if it's smaller than you'd like and when we break in we will have Mes, and the other women and Tommy. Together we can save everyone."

"I can't do this Stuart, I'm not John."

In frustration, I reply, "No, you're not. Not like this. And I think he would be ashamed to see you this way."

He doesn't flinch in anger or express any recognition of what I just said. His expression doesn't change - it stays showing that same look of self-pity and shame. This is not good. He does not acknowledge me. He does not yell back or say anything cutting. He merely stands up and slowly walks towards the door past Sarah who is now standing there.

“And what about Mes? Are you going to leave your own sister? She would give everything to bring you back and you’re just going to turn your back on her?” I yell at him, but he carries on until he is gone.

Sarah slowly comes to me.

“How could he give up like that,” I snarl.

“He hasn't given up Stuart.”

“Yes, he has. Did you not see him just now? We've lost him.”

“No, you haven’t,” she explains calmly. “He’s just hurting. Being a leader isn't easy. His feelings are all over the place at the moment. You are no longer like them Stuart, yes, we feel, but we concentrate on one emotion at a time. And right now, you are focused on Kimmy, just Kimmy nothing else, and all you desire is to get her back. He doesn't know it yet, but he is in control and he will be ready. Humans just need time. You seem to have forgotten about that already.”

She is right and she says it kindly enough. I had almost forgotten what it is like to be human. My key focus is Kimmy as it will always be and always had been, but my care for others could not fade as well else I could become like our enemies.

“But we don't have that much time.”

“Let me worry about Alex for now. I am betting your father will be more upset if you leave him waiting any longer.”

I believe that to be true. My father was a kind and gentle man, but I could tell from the gym that he has a side to him you wouldn’t want to unleash, so I do as she says and hurry outside, forgetting Alex for now.

And when I get there, I almost laugh at the sight of him, standing there drenched from head to toe, his face a mask.

“Did you get lost or something?”

“Sorry,” I say the laughter slipping out. “Had to take a short detour.” I tell him of what just happened with Alex, and he pretty much said the same as Sarah, “give him a little bit more time” he ended it with.

He stiffened up “This is serious. You need to feed. You don't need human blood but blood is still needed, or you become weak and therefore can lose control of who you are.”

I already heard the same kind of story from Nathaniel, while he was trying to get me to feed on humans.

“You need to learn to hunt animals. It’s the only way to stay strong without feeding on humans.”

Looking at the seriousness of my father’s face, I can see that this isn't a laughing matter. He doesn't want me losing control and attacking innocents, and neither do I.

“You don't want the blood of innocents on your hands, son, you will never forget them,” he says looking away from me, his voice laden with disappointment.

“Even the strongest of us have lost control, and the pain it causes can force you to turn off your emotions - it becomes easier to let the beast take over because then you won't feel the pain of loss. Nothing will hurt you but you are no longer yourself, just an emotionless soul. You don't want that. Nobody does.”

I look at him properly, watching as he ponders, lost in thought. I can't picture my father being what he describes, but I wonder if someone close to him had done this, had let go of everything and became the monster. His face is a picture of hurt. I can't ask. I don't want to force him to linger on his bad memories.

"So, shall we do this?" I say to bring him back to reality and out of whatever nightmare he is reliving.

After we treed deep into the woods, my father stops me and perches on a huge rock and beckons me to continue.

"What?" I ask in a whisper.

"I want you to continue alone. Use your senses, all of them, smell, hearing, vision. Find your animal and procure it, or you do not eat tonight."

I can feel that my body is in desperate need of feeding, my stomach churns and my muscles had been aching since I awoke so I do as he tells me. I lurked further through the woods as quiet as I can until my father is no longer in sight. I try to listen, to concentrate, but the wind is heavy and the rain splashes to the ground taking away my full concentration. With my new hearing, the drops sound like small bombs as they crash to the floor. I run my eyes through the trees looking for any movement. It is pitch black but it does not affect my eyes anymore. I can see for hundreds of meters as clear as it were day. But I still see nothing alive.

Time passes and I lean up against a huge old tree and slump my body against it, calming myself. The wind gently turns direction, pushing the rain away. The rustling of leaves and the creaking of branches grows quieter. For a few seconds, the sound of the rain likewise dies down and it is silent, dead silent. In that space, I hear a light thud from behind me. I spin around to try to find it. I peer through the trees and flickering across my eyes I see a hare sprinting through the woods. My nostrils flare and I can smell the blood racing through its body, almost able to taste it. Without hesitation, I spring to my feet and shoot off like a dart, gliding through the air and brushing past the branches, gaining on the hare with every step. I see its eyes flicker my way, its heart pounds faster and it speeds up. I can feel its fear as I continue to gain on it. I am a predator hunting and the hare knows that. It twists and turns as it tries to find safety, a hole or something where it could leap into, out of my reach. My urge to feed only makes me faster, and my reflexes grow with every turn. I am able to dart in a new direction as smoothly and quickly as a bat through the air. I can sense every sudden movement it makes, every attempt to spring into a new direction. Without a second thought, I throw myself at the hare and, clenching one leg with my fingers, I hear as its leg snaps and the cry it makes. It's horrible.

It makes me feel sorry for the poor creature. The fear the hare feels runs through me like it is my own emotion. The little creature's fear of death almost brings tears to my eyes but better him than a human. I can't let it suffer any more so with a quick bite to its neck the pain stops and the hare stills. The emotions of the hare which I was tapping into faded away, the warm blood flows into my mouth and down my gullet. From there I can feel it fill my body. The taste is amazing. It tastes much better than I would have imagined. Squeezing the life out of it to get every last drop, I finally feel fuller, stronger. The aches have all disappeared. Once I have swallowed every last drop, I let the body go and stand up. Now I can sense everything; my senses are ten times more sensitive than they were just mere moments ago. It dawns on me just how weak my body had been. I had been a lurker for almost a week and not fed once. I feel invincible. If I could nearly defeat Claire running on empty, how would she manage against me with my body fully loaded and stronger than ever. In every direction I can now hear the scurrying of little paws and chirps and squeaks. The noises hit me like sirens and I suddenly have my pick of them all. I waste no more time.

Three more hares and a delicious fox later, I gather myself together, feeling that my body was fully fed and in top shape. I wipe the drips of blood leaking down my chin and try to listen out for sounds of my father to locate him. The rain had slowed and grown thin as I hunted. The heavy drops had become a small shower. I pick up a scent which is not from the animals but neither does it belong to my father. It's that awful smell of death and dried blood and it's stronger than ever. I spin my head in every direction, trying to pin point it, but this is no singular scent. I am surrounded.

Suddenly men from all around fly out of the bushes and trees. And equally as suddenly, out of nowhere a tree trunk flies across and takes out three men. We, my attackers and I, as one look in the direction it came from and there is my father outside the circle, ready to defend me. Without hesitation, I sprint in the direction of the five men that are left. They arch their bodies and growl, ready for what is coming. My father reaches them before me and immediately takes two men out of the game. I am stopped by one who flings himself on top of me, punching me in my face as he does so. He has a lot of strength. After a few blows to the face, I finally get a hand free and drive it into his chest, winding him and sending him skidding off me and into a nearby tree. He quickly breaks a branch off and snaps it until it resembles a wooden stake. He throws himself at me. Time seems to slow and I have time to grab a stone from the ground and slash it across his face mid-air sending him crashing to the ground. I grab his arm and dislocate it. I then swipe the stake out of his hand, spin him over and just as I am about to thrust the stake into his heart, "ENOUGH" another one shouts from behind with a growl so loud it frightens nearby birds which all flee their nests and stops us all mid fight.

"We did not come here to fight," he continued.

This man seems familiar. I take a moment to place him and then remember this man had been one of Nathaniel's bodyguards, who stood by the door when Nathaniel first took me to his dining area for our so-called chat. He was one of the men who brought Mr Fisher in all beaten and half dead. Realizing this, I do not release the one I have in my grips and my father had already dispatched of two of the men but the other two lie beaten on the ground at his feet.

"And why should we believe you?" my father snarls at the guard.

"Because we're here with a message, for him," he says, pointing towards me. "Nathaniel would like for you to join him once again, for a chat," he says with a flash of a cheeky smile. It's neither friendly nor comforting.

My father starts laughing before he can even finish his sentence.

"Well that's just great. I should kill you all right now for delivering such an idiotic message."

I jump in at this point agreeing with my father that this is a ridiculous request. "You can tell Nathaniel-"

But before I can finish, he jumps in again. "I won't be telling Nathaniel anything. Apart from delivering you to him that is for you to tell him yourself," he says. He is so confident that I will be going with him despite all the evidence to the contrary. There must be something else. I look back at my father, confused.

He quickly punches one of the lurkers at his feet who is just coming around and then comes to stand beside me.

"My son is going nowhere. If you would like to try and take him, feel free to try."

The man looks at the men he brought with him, their bodies lying scattered around us but still his expression does not change. "There will be no need for me to try to take him. You both will be coming of your own free will."

"Both?" I repeat.

"Yes, both. We can't have your daddy running back and telling your people where you are now, can we?"

"Well I don't think he will be doing either, seeing as we are done here."

We begin to walk away but the man's voice rises up, "well I guess poor Kimmy is going to be put on the menu after all."

My whole body stiffens at this mention of her name. He continues, "I can't wait to sink my teeth into that one. So young, so beautiful."

Suddenly my body flushes with anger and fear and I grip the stake harder; with one swift turn, I throw the stake which pierces the man's shoulder. Before he can say anything else, I have a hold of him and am pressing him up against the nearest tree.

"You will not do anything," I scream uncontrollably. "Do you hear me? I will tear your fucking head off." I throw my fist into his face, force him to his knees and tug on his head, trying to make my threat a reality. Fear runs over the man's face as he looks into my eyes. I can only imagine that for him, my eyes look full of blackness and horror because he starts screaming for his life.

"If you kill me you will never see her!"

But I do not listen, I only pull harder, any reasoning having left me. The realization that Nathaniel now knows who Kimmy is and has her at his mercy has taken over me and has left me uncontrollably fearing for her life. I only want to destroy this man who had brought this upon me.

But before I can tear his head from his body, my father's hands grab mine, prise me off the lurker guard and then I too am flung up against the tree. I can see the emotion in my father's eyes - the sorrow, the regret of having to do such a thing, the determination and conviction that he has to.

"Stop son, stop. He will kill her!" he shouts as I try to break free to continue to break this man apart.

I eventually stop fighting as the anger passes into pain and drains me of the extra strength. I want to give in to every emotion and just to break down on my father's shoulder and cry out all the pain. To let it all out rather than having it running through my body in my veins, to exorcise all the images running through my mind. But I cannot do that in front of the enemy. He knows as I slump that he has us. We both look at him as he removes the stake from his shoulder and watch the smile grow across his face as the injuries on his neck began to heal. He knows he has us right where he wanted us: alone and totally at their mercy.

Chapter 17

Alex was sat down on his bed, his eyes red, clearly having been sobbing. His head sprung up when he heard a sudden knock on the door. Sarah stood there, pity written across her face. He met her gaze for a moment but then dropped his head in shame.

She walked over and planted herself on the bed beside him. "What's the problem, Alex?"

He looked up at her again. "What do you mean?"

"I mean why are you sitting here alone instead of being out there, taking control of your own men? Because I know it has nothing to do with not been capable."

"I am not capable, I proved that back at the camp."

"From what I heard, you were taken by surprise, they attacked in force and that had nothing to do with you."

"Yes it did. I chose to open the doors. I chose to lead the men out there, and now..."

He stopped and tried to hold back the tears that threatened to burst out of him, like a river of emotions. He was thinking about how he lost his mentor, the man who saved him and his sister when everything had started to go wrong, who had taught them how to protect themselves, taught them how to survive. And, in one quick decision that he, Alex, had made, he had failed him.

"You don't understand. John protested against opening the doors and I ignored him. I forced him to open the doors, believing I could help. But I only made things worse. We lost everything, our men, our friends, John, my sister."

Sarah cut him off before he could carry on blaming himself for everything.

"And none of that is your fault. You made a decision to help out a friend.

Stuart was about to die, as well as Richard, and you saved them. Yes, you lost men, you lost people you care about, but there are still friends and family alive now, scared and alone and they are trapped by those same people who took everything from you. They need your help, Alex. And your men here need your help. They won't follow me, or Stuart, or any of us. They need you. As much as you blame yourself for what happened, nobody else does. In a war like this, there are decisions you make and battles you lose. No one can make a decision which saves everyone."

He looked into the abyss while taking in what Sarah told him, but time passed and his look of self-pity did not change. Sarah stood up and walked to the door to leave but slowly turned back to Alex as she thought of something else to add.

"Look Alex, I am not going to sit here telling you something you already know, but Stuart and Richard are going to demand that we attack them soon, and when that time comes, we're going to need you and your men."

She walked out of the room and down the hall, making her way to the front of the house. She asked a few guards on the way if Richard and Stuart had returned yet but none of them knew anything. She felt a sudden discomfort as she searched the rooms, looking for the two of them, and when they were nowhere to be seen, she continued her search out of the house, taking a few trackers with her. She trailed through the woods looking for clues about any direction they may have taken, but she only came across a few dead animals that had their life source drained from them. After a few more minutes had past, she heard one of the guards shout that he had found something. She quickly made her way there to join him. She suddenly came to a stop as she saw two of Nathaniel's men lying on the ground, dead. The trackers told her what her own sense of smell had picked up, that there had been more people here and a group, including Richard had set off in the same direction. They were gone. Dread took over her.

Chapter 18

We come to where the woods thin out and across the adjoining field I can see a small estate, rows of houses and buildings block after block. Towering over the houses is a huge building seeming to be in the middle resembles a huge factory of sorts. As we cross the field and near the estate, my fear grows with every step. I have no idea what we will walk in to see, if Kimmy will even be alive, or even if she is alive, will they allow her to stay that way after they have me and my father contained. I hope Sarah has noticed that we hadn't returned but with Alex out of commission unable to lead his men, the numbers would be against them if they were to attempt a rescue mission.

We walk through the estate and house after house is empty. There is not a sound except our footsteps and their uncanny echoes. Every now and again, I look at my father and he gives me a nod of security. I know it is stupid to believe that we could get through this but having my father next to me helps.

We turn a few corners and finally the huge building looms up ahead of us. It turns out to be an old clothes factory; I can see the outline of where the 'next' letters used to hang. We stop by a huge metal gate. The lead guard stares into a camera perched at top of a pole beside the gate. After a few moments, the gates rattle, then suddenly begin opening. The noise permeates the whole area, echoing and rumbling, which only serves to make the whole scene more terrifying. The guards push me and my father through the gate, and all I can think about is how much of a fort this building is. They have picked the perfect place; it's far more impenetrable than the mansion. Metal fences surround the whole area. There are few entrances and each are accompanied by several guards and automatic metal shutters, much like the ones at the camp. I can see more guards watching us from the windows, of which there are very few. There will not be an easy way out. We pass through the car park and up to the only door I can see which might be penetrable for an attack - it is a reception area with glass doors which would be easy to break through, but yet again there are at least ten guards surrounding the entrance, armed with guns.

We are forced through this front entrance and into the reception area. I should have expected it but I still get a jolt of shock and horror to see Claire sat down, legs crossed, on the sofa in the lobby, looking as stunning as ever. Her long black hair falls like silk dropping to her waist and hanging over her shoulders; her eyes are as dark as the night. Once again, she is smiling broadly, that evil smile of triumph. She raises herself from the seat and confronts my father, still smiling but right up in his face.

"You have no idea how happy I am to see you here, Richard!" she says gleefully.

He does not respond. Her glee fades a little. She quickly turns her attention to me. "Ahhhh Stuart. I believe we have someone that belongs to you."

Without either hesitation or threat, I raise my voice, "If she is hurt in any way, Claire, I swear, I will tear you apart."

She must see the determination in my eyes. For a brief second, her smile fully drops but she recuperates it quickly. “Bring them through,” she orders the guards.

She sets off walking and the guards once again shove us forward, forcing us to follow Claire up some stairs to the second floor. We walk down a hall with a few doors on either side and I can hear the sounds of machinery through the walls but by the time we reach the last door the noise has vanished. She opens the door and steps through. We follow in to find Nathaniel standing behind a desk, looking out of the window into the night sky. He doesn’t change from this position as we walk in.

I quickly scan the room looking for Kimmy, trying to catch her scent but Nathaniel cuts me off.

“She's not in here Stuart,” he says in a mocking tone, leering at me with a death-defying stare that suddenly reminds me how terrifying he is. He notices my father beside me and his face instantly switches from evil smile to absolute hatred.

“Richard, you must be able to guess my feelings of shock and delight when Claire told me about your relation to Stuart. You must understand the joy it will bring me to cut you down from that high and mighty branch you have built for yourself over the centuries.”

My father’s face is tense, his jaw working, grinding from side to side.

“What do you want with my son, Nathaniel?” he angrily forces the words out.

Nathaniel doesn’t answer but instead places his hands on the top rail of two chairs on our side of the desk. He towers of us, beckoning us to take a seat. After a long and tense stare off between Nathaniel and my father, my father decides to take the offered seat. There is no chance of escape at this moment in time, and my father knows that better than anyone. Nathaniel is as old and as strong as my father, maybe stronger. I hope to god that is not the case, but just in this room, we would have to fight him and three other men plus Claire who is conveniently blocking the door behind us. We are for all purposes outnumbered and overpowered.

He takes a seat in front of us as we lower ourselves into our seats. He spreads his arms across the desk and entwine his fingers together. Everything is calculated to intimidate us and create a picture of evil.

"Forgive me, but I really am lost for words to finally have you here, Richard. Although of course, you are most welcome. After all, we have been at war for going on six centuries, have we not? I must admit, this is a very proud moment for me. And to find out that you have a son, who I once had in my possession just makes this story's ending that all much tastier."

I can see the power-mad look in his eyes. After all, he and my father have been at war longer than most of us in this room can even believe, and this monster is going to make every bit count. It just makes sense to me that with this as the case, there is no way we will be leaving this building alive.

"Where is Kimmy?" I blurt out, interrupting his reminiscing over the years he had battled my father, and I can see the immediate frustration in his face as I do so. But it does not matter to me; I have to see her, I have to make sure they haven't hurt her.

His nostrils flare as I stare him down. In this, he resembles my father whose nostrils have been flared the whole time we have been here.

"You will see her in time, Stuart," he calmly says. But there is nothing calm about my own emotions and I am not going to let this go. I need to see her.

"Please, I need to know she's ok. Take me to her."

"You are not in a place to be giving demands, Stuart!" his voice grows stronger and angrier as his face grows straighter and tighter. "You are lucky she is still alive after the trouble you brought my way."

"Why was he there in the first place, Nathaniel? You had no use for him."

Nathaniel's face becomes calm again as my father speaks.

"Now that isn't true. Is it Richard?"

I look at my father to see if he understands, but his face, like mine, is a picture of confusion.

"You have spent enough time with him by now to realize he is not like us. One so young should never be able to control as he does. He has the strength of one ten times his age. No, Richard, you know he's different."

"He is strong, yes. It does not mean that he is different. You have no use for him. Let my son and Kimmy go. You have me. They are no threat to you."

"If only that were true! But you know if I am lenient one day, I will die the next. You will both die here. It's such a shame, you would be a great pupil Stuart, if only you could release that beast inside you."

A grim smile appears around his face, as he nods to one of the guards. The guard reacts quickly and leaves the room. This is all rehearsed.

"Let's see if we can make that happen, shall we?"

"Wait," my father interjects. "Nathaniel, don't."

"What's the matter, Richard? This used to be a favourite sport, did it not?"

“Not this, Nathaniel, please. Not my son. Let me do it. If I break, you can have me.”

“Don't be foolish. I know better than to wager against you. Plus, this way I don’t have to kill him. And after a bit of training, Stuart will become my strongest soldier. He will be spared.”

“Nathaniel, I swear to you, I will-”

But before my father can finish his sentence, Nathaniel launches himself over the desk and slams his fist into my father’s face, with such force that it shakes the whole room and almost sends my father off the chair.

“YOU WILL WHAT?” his face glares with the rush of anger which fills his face. His eyes shine brighter the angrier he gets.

“You would be dead before you get the chance to do anything. The only reason you are still alive is because I want to see your face as you see your son become every bit the monster you used to be. Then Richard, we will let you die.”

I know I should be afraid of whatever is coming. My father had showed no emotion, no fear regarding our situation until now. And if he is scared, then I should be too, but all my emotions are concentrated on Kimmy.

Suddenly the guard comes back in. I was expecting him to be dragging Kimmy in but he returns empty-handed and just makes the slightest nod to Nathaniel. Then he grabs me, pulls me from my chair while two others grab my father. They force us out of the door and back into the corridor, pushing us down a twisted set of stairs to the bottom floor. Nathaniel and Claire follow leisurely behind. Then we enter through another door which leads us even further down into a cellar. The further down we get, the louder the bangs become. They are mixed into echoes of cheers and roars, vibrations of banging and shaking. We reach the bottom of the stairs and a narrow old stone walk way is in front of us. At the end is the roaring, the cheering and a beam of light. They force us down the walkway. The screams have become so loud in my head that I have to adjust my hearing so that my eardrums don't explode.

We come into the light at the end of the walk way and find ourselves in a pit, surrounded by dozens of lurkers crowded around it, rattling the cages around the edge of the pit. They scream louder as we enter. I look at my father, unable to suppress my fear now and he drops his head. Nathaniel and Claire's faces are glowing with excitement. As they enter, the lurkers scream to them as if they are a king and queen.

Nathaniel waves his hand and they all gradually quieten.

"My young ones," he says. "The main event is here! The one we have been waiting for!"

As they all restart their cheering and inhuman whooping, I am forced forward onto my knees in the middle of the pit. Everyone else walks over to some stairs surrounded by cages at the side and walk up to a balcony over viewing the whole pit: my father, Nathaniel, Claire and three guards. They seat themselves above me. My father is fighting but the three guards strike him every time he tries to break free.

I stand up and the crowd lowers.

"What the hell is this Nathaniel? Where's Kimmy?"

"This is where you have to decide."

I look around in confusion, my whole body tense and anxious. "Decide what?"

"Your future," he says as he gestures to one of the men at another end of the room. He grabs a huge rope and tugs on it. This opens a huge metal door at the other end of the pit, revealing two lurkers with huge, red-gleaming eyes, and fangs piercing out of their mouths, saliva dripping. They remind me of the first lurker Kimmy and I came across, the one who attacked us in the cabin. The rabidity and rage-filled look on his face is a spitting image of these two.

That's when understanding hits and I know my fate - Nathaniel wants me to fight, he wants me to lose control and become like him, emotionless and careless. What kind of monster can own a place like this, let alone welcome the death that comes with it? Now I notice all the dried bloodstains and the old rusted shackles nailed to the sides. This is more than a fighting pit. Another door open and out come some more lurkers who force two girls out, humans, naked and skin torn, bleeding from all their limbs, screaming and in pain. My eyes fill up and I can't repress the tears. I can feel their fear so strongly, read their faces - all they want is their parents. They can't be older than fifteen and they are both uncontrollably crying and screaming.

They are quickly shackled to either side of the pit and these latest lurkers leave, shutting the doors behind them, then the crowd once again quietens and they all look at Nathaniel, even the crazy rabid ones in the pit with me.

Time suddenly slows down for me, so slowly it almost stops as I turn to watch Nathaniel too. I see the awful excitement on his face, and he nods his head, excruciatingly slowly. As I turn back, time suddenly speeds back up and I watch in horror as they sprint to one girl and sink their fangs teeth into her neck. The battles had been bad enough but this is something else. I'm rooted to the spot in horror. I can only watch, and listen. The screams from her and her friend, the horrible noises being made as they tear into her. I cannot move. This is a sight only straight from a horror movie. It makes the memory of the woman back in the mansion much lighter.

I am thrown fully back into reality as blood suddenly sprays across my face. The smell is invigorating so close to my nostrils as I breathe it in, but I fight that urge and force myself to look at the horror before me. I should witness this for their sakes even as the girl's limbs are torn off and her screams stop and I feel nauseous. I stand still and stiff, but suddenly I notice an itch down my cheek. I slowly wipe it away and notice it is a tear. I rub my eyes and face trying to remove the blood, then I notice one of the lurkers stand up leaving the other still feeding. He careers towards the other girl, who is backed up against the wall, crying and screaming for him to stay away, begging as he closes in.

Suddenly my feet react, my body starts boiling with that familiar feeling which spreads from my feet all the way to my head and burning as it does so. I breathe in to prepare, tensing my body and then leap towards him as he goes to grab the girl. I fling myself on top of him, grabbing him by his throat, picking him up and throwing him into the wall. I grab the shackle attached to the wall next to him and fasten it around his throat. As I tug harder, he lets out a high-pitched primordial scream which cuts off abruptly when his head detaches from his body.

Just then the other realizes what I have done. He leaves the corpse of the dead girl and rampages towards me. It's my turn to be thrown against the wall. My body goes numb from the impact as he throws me across the pit once more and I land next to the puddle that was once a living girl. He powers towards me again and throws his arms around my neck, twisting it as hard as he can. I am stronger than him though and can still reach down and grab the shackles on the floor and cave the hard iron into his face which forces him to let me go. I pummel his head into the wall and grab the back of his neck and tear with all the strength I have until once again I detach his head from his body.

Battle over, I take measure of my surroundings again. The crowd is silent again. I look at Nathaniel and his face is austere. There is no hint of a smile left.

“I don't know what you are expecting to achieve from this, Nathaniel. This,” I gesture at the pit, the cage and the dead girl, “only makes me hate you more.”

“Don’t abandon hope, Stuart. We will find a way to bring out that beast in you. BRING HER IN,” he orders in a bellow which rattles the metal of the cage.

My heart stops. I look at the man beside the rope again who opens the door. A lurker charged through and throws somebody into the pit. Before she can smash into the floor, I fly towards her and catch her in my arms. The woman cowers in my arms, crying without looking up. Tears stream out of my eyes, even before I muster the strength to move her hair out of her face. As I do, she slowly looks up at me, terrified, but she stops sobbing as she sees my face. It is Kimmy. My heart is struck with pain as soon as I see her face.

“Stuart?” she says gently. I can see the force it takes her to try to raise a smile meeting me in this circumstance. She raises her hand and wipes my cheek, gently removing the splatters of blood. “You’re here,” she says even more gently than the first time. Her tears are now mixed with tears of joy at seeing me. I squeeze her so tight as I feel my heart speed up and my body shake with happiness from being reunited despite our predicament. Right now, there is no one here but us. I lay my head on her forehead.

“I'm here.”

But I am jolted back into this horrific situation as my father screams something forcing me to look up.

Lurkers are piling in the pit, flying towards me. I spin around and take a blow from the first lurker which sends both Kimmy and I diving across the pit. I move myself in mid-air so that she lands on top of me, breaking her fall. Once again, her face is full of fear, as she sees the lurkers coming towards us. The idea of what had just happened to the other poor girl happening to Kimmy is my worst nightmare. The picture triggers a reaction unlike any other. My body becomes hard, my mind becomes blank, my eyesight goes red as blood itself, my fangs grow so large they prick my own lips. I have no fear. I must protect Kimmy. I will die before I see them touch Kimmy.

I keep Kimmy and the young girl behind me, jump to my feet, stretch out my arms and claw my fingers as if they are talons, like an eagle grabbing its prey. I let out a long growl, a growl so loud, so shaking that the whole crowd stops, which I register just at the edge of my consciousness. The lurkers running towards us hesitate. The whole room is silent. For a split second, I feel the fear, palpably in the room, in everybody but myself. Nathaniel now stands, eyes as wide and excited as ever. I hear his voice say "there it is". My father shakes his head but I no longer care. I just know I have to stop whoever wants to hurt Kimmy. And then, when she is safe, I will tear Nathaniel's head from his body for putting her in danger.

Nathaniel nods again and suddenly the lurkers hiss in unison and continue their attack, but I move so fast they cannot touch me. Every strike I land breaks bones and sends our attackers flying to the ground in pain. Strike after strike, I pile through them. There is blood splattered all over my face.

Suddenly the ground shakes and the shaking cracks the floor. This jolts me back to myself as I join everybody looking up at the roof above us. We all hear gunshots followed by screams echoing in the corridors outside this arena.

Suddenly one of the top doors slams open and Sarah comes marching through leading her band of lurkers who charge through the crowd fighting and slaying as they move forward. Then the opposite door opens with a storm of gunfire and Alex leads his men into the fray. All the screams, howls and gunfire ricochet off the walls and echo causing such a din. My senses are overwhelmed.

In the chaos and confusion, I hear my father scream my name. As I look towards him where he is winning against a group of guards, I notice that Nathaniel and Claire are nowhere to be seen. My father, in between blows, signals towards the walk-through. Then I notice that Kimmy is gone.

Without hesitating, I sprint through the walk through and clear the steps in a few bounds. I run through the building, hall after hall, screaming out for Kimmy. The fight has escaped the top floor now and the building has become a battlefield. I ignore the lurkers and the humans, the gunfire, the screams, the bodies, the blows. No one touches me and I run straight through aiming for the exit.

I reach the car park to find a truck piling out through the gates. Suddenly I see a flash from the rooftop and before I can scream it hits the car - a rocket launcher blowing the truck onto its side. I run down to the car reaching it in mere seconds. I pull the burning truck back upright but there is nobody in it.

I look around the street trying my hardest to spot Kimmy, letting out a whimper at the very thought of losing her like this. I spot her further down the road where she has been flung yards from the car. This hits me like a brick to the face, but suddenly I find myself crushed into the wall as Nathaniel has me in his grip. I look into his evil face and watch as his burns begin to heal and fade.

"You shall watch as she dies, you absolutely insignificant worm. You have brought me nothing."

His grip is so tight, so powerful compared to any other lurker. I can see Kimmy in my mind's eye, lying there on the floor, fading away. I can't fight him off.

Suddenly he is lifted off his feet and crashes to the floor, with my father on top of him. He throws my father off him with ease, grabs a piece of shrapnel from the explosion and sticks it through my father's chest. This spurs me back into action before Nathaniel can finish my father off. I scream a war cry and sprint towards him. As he turns to me with a huge smile on his face, I throw my hand into his chest. Suddenly his smile turns to shock, then confusion. He looks down, open mouthed. My rage calms and suddenly I can feel what he can see - my hand has penetrated his chest. I push harder until I can squeeze, until I can squeeze the one thing that keeps Nathaniel alive. I process this fact but don't think any further. With one quick tug I pull it from his chest cavity and drop it on the floor. He makes a noise in his throat as if to say something but nothing distinguishable comes out as he drops down, crumpled, to the ground as life-less as his soul had always been.

"Stuart!" my father shouts pointing towards Kimmy.

I run over to her body, turn her over and almost throw up. Her face is burned badly, her pulse is faint and slow, her breathing is ragged. She looks me in the eyes as she lies dying, but she only smiles.

"No, no, no! Please don't go! Don't leave me Kimmy! Please!" I beg as she rolls her eyes and falls unconscious. My face shudders and my eyes grow heavy and fill up.

A man screams in pain and I turn to see Alex and Mes carrying Tommy towards us. They place him on the floor, a metre or so from where we lie. My whole body shakes as I let out a huge scream and sob so hard it hurts my face, squeezing her in my arms, rocking both our bodies, with nothing but pain running through me.

"Bite her."

I hear the words. They filter through my pain and grief, tantalizingly close to making sense. They pull at my consciousness. And then their force hits and brings my head up in shock. My father is crawling up to us. "Listen to her heart," he tells me. "She's still alive. Bite her, Stuart."

I hesitate not knowing what to do.

"Son you don't have long. Bite her."

I look to Tommy and he nods in agreement as he wipes the tears off his face. "Do it, do it now, Stuart," he urges.

Turning her against her will would be wrong. Who knows how she would be when she woke. Every fibre in my body knows it is wrong. She could become a monster, no longer the woman I loved. She might not turn out like me and my father. But I am not ready to lose her. The risk has to be worth it. Before I do anything, I already feel the regret, but the vision of having her wake up, being able to hold her again, hear her voice again is too overpowering.

So I bend down, gently push my fangs into her neck, and try to inject the venom into her bloodstream as fast as I possibly can.

To be continued.

Printed in Great Britain
by Amazon